Truth,
Dare, Kiss,
Promise

Midsummer Meltdown

Cathy Hopkins lives in London with her husband and two cats, Emmylou and Otis. The cats appear to be slightly insane. Their favourite game is to run from one side of the house to the other as fast as possible, then see if they can fly if they leap high enough off the furniture. This is usually at three o'clock in the morning and they land on anyone who happens to be asleep at the time.

Cathy spends most of her time locked in a shed at the bottom of the garden pretending to write books but is actually in there listening to music, hippie dancing and checking her Facebook page.

Apart from that, Cathy has joined the gym and spends more time than is good for her making up excuses as to why she hasn't got time to go.

Cathy Hopkins

Midsummer Meltdown

Piccadilly Press • London

Thanks to Brenda Gardner, Jon Appleton, Melissa Patey and all the team at Piccadilly. Thanks as always to Rosemary Bromley, my lovely agent, sadly no longer with us. And to Steve Lovering for his constant support and help in researching all aspects of this book.

First published in Great Britain in 2005
by Piccadilly Press Ltd,
5 Castle Road, London NW1 8PR

This edition published 2008

Text copyright © Cathy Hopkins, 2005

A catalogue record for this book is available from the British Library

ISBN: 978 1 85340 972 1 (paperback)

3 5 7 9 10 8 6 4 2

Printed in

Secrets and Lies

SQUIDGE NARROWED HIS EYES and scrutinised me closely as if he was trying to read my mind. 'Something's going on with you, Lia Axford,' he said after a while. 'There's something you're not telling us.'

Cat, Becca and Mac turned away from the horror DVD we were watching to join Squidge in staring at me.

'Rubbish,' I said. 'There's nothing going on.' I tried to look him straight in the eyes as I said this but it was difficult because he was right. Something was going on. Or would be going on some time soon. The weekend after next, to be precise. But I couldn't tell anybody. Not yet. My dad had made me promise.

'Is there?' asked Becca as she popped a salt and vinegar crisp into her mouth. 'Is something going on?'

I folded my arms across my stomach and crossed my

legs. 'Yeah. A movie,' I said as I turned my attention back to the TV screen. 'And we're missing it.'

'Whoa,' said Mac. 'Get a load of Lia's body language. A dead give-away. She's closed right off. I saw a programme about it on telly last week. Your body says what your mouth doesn't.'

I quickly uncrossed my arms and legs. 'All my body is trying to say is that I'm not keen on this movie. I don't like scary films but you guys carry on, I know you like them. Anyone want more drinks? Crisps?'

I got up to go out of the room but Squidge dived on to the floor and caught my right ankle. 'We don't want to watch any more until you tell us what's happening,' he insisted as I almost toppled over. 'I know something is, and remember, body language or no body language, I can go beyond that. I-I-I-I can r-e-e-e-e-ad your m-i-i-i-i-nd.'

I felt myself go pink because, a few moments earlier when he was staring at me, I was thinking that if only I could get rid of the others, we could have a snogging session instead of getting freaked out by some stupid, scary movie. Cat, Becca and Mac might be my best mates down here in Cornwall but Squidge is more than a mate. He's my boyfriend and possibly the most romantic boy in the world, but I hadn't been on my own with him for ages. I hadn't said anything because I didn't want to be too demanding or come across as clingy. I'd read in one of Becca's magazines that boys don't like that and that it's best to give them space – plus, he seemed to be enjoying the film. My brother Ollie left it for us to watch before he went back to his school up in London last night. He loves this kind of thing and thinks that whatever he likes everyone else will too. I don't, but I was outvoted by the others. Getting scared out of my wits is not my idea of fun. I can just about sit through a horror film when there are people around, but they come back to haunt me later. Seriously. In the middle of the night when I'm alone in my room, it's then that the most frightening part of the movie starts to play back in my head. I imagine eyes watching me in the dark, hands appearing outside the window trying to get in, headless bodies floating about in the corridors, coming through the walls to hover over my bed. Sometimes I have to put the covers over my head as I reckon if I can't see them, they can't see me.

'Actually, you can't read minds because you haven't a clue what I was thinking. And *nothing* is going on,' I lied.

Squidge laughed. 'Your name is Lia, not liar. You are the worst liar in the world.'

Mac pressed the pause button on the remote control and the DVD froze on the screen with some girl in mid-scream.

'Right,' he said. 'Spill. If my mate says you are holding back on us, then you are holding back on us.'

Four pairs of eyes stared at me. Mac's. Becca's. Cat's. Squidge's. Almost like a scene from the DVD. They're a good-looking bunch normally but each of them can pull a freaky face when they want – a face they'd practised in the 'who can do the grossest face?' competition that we like to play from time to time. Cat ran her fingers through her short, dark hair, making it stick up like she'd just got out of bed, and made herself go cross-eyed. Mac flattened his straw-blond hair and pulled his lips in so that it looked like he had no mouth. Becca pulled her Titian-red hair over her face so that it was like a curtain obscuring all her features except for her tongue which she poked through the hair, and Squidge did the same as Cat and spiked his dark hair up like a mad man's, then stuck his front teeth over his bottom lip.

'Stop it,' I said. 'Stop looking at me like that. It's spooking me out.'

Squidge began to cackle and laugh as if he was possessed and then he got up and started walking like a zombie from the film. Mac got up too, followed by Becca and Cat and soon they were all walking round the room acting like they had no brains. And they were coming towards me.

Cat, Becca, Mac and Squidge have been my mates since I decided to change from my boarding school in London to the local school down here in Cornwall last September. Not that boarding school was bad or that I didn't like London because I did. In fact, my sister Star lives up there in Notting Hill and my brother Ollie wasn't far away at his school in Kensington. Thing was, I missed my parents and I missed being at home. I felt like I was always travelling. It took forty minutes to get from my old school to Paddington station, three hours from Paddington to Plymouth, then it's a forty-minute drive to where we live. The quickest way to get here is actually by helicopter and sometimes Dad hires one, because we have a landing pad down here behind the paddocks at the back of the house. But mainly it was the train on Friday night or Saturday morning and then I'd have to leave mid-afternoon on Sunday to be back in time for school on Monday.

I'm so much happier now. It's like I have a normal life – well, as normal as it ever will be for the Axford family. My dad is rock star Zac Axford. He was famous in the Eighties and still has a devoted following, although Ollie and I tease him that he belongs more to the ageing rock star category. My mum is/was Carly Newman, top model in America until she married Dad and gave it all up to be a mother. My sister is Star Axford, also top model and featured on just about every front cover of every glossy at the moment. My brother Ollie is still at school but no doubt he'll go on to do something fab and glam as he's already heading that way. He was Romeo in his school's production of *Romeo and Juliet* last year and he definitely has charisma, a fact that he's well aware of. Even I can see that he is a babe magnet. And then there's me. People say I'm the quiet one, sometimes I think that actually they mean the ordinary one. If it weren't for the fact that I clearly have my mum's hair (blond) and flat chest (all the Axford girls have size AA boobs) and Dad's eyes (silver blue), I'd say that I was from a different family altogether. People say that I'm good-looking but I don't think I am. I think my neck's too long, I'm too bony-looking and on a bad day I look like a duck! I don't have any super-duper musical talents like Dad. I can't act like Ollie and I don't like being the centre of attention like Star. I don't even know what I want to do when I leave school yet. Perhaps be a vet, but I'm not sure. Not knowing is starting to worry me as we had to choose GCSE subjects earlier this year for when we go into Year Ten next September, and I'm not sure I picked the right ones.

'Tell us the truth or you'll become a zombie like us,' said Squidge in a deep voice.

'Never,' I said. 'My secrets will die with me.'

Mac hovered over where I'd fallen back on the sofa when Squidge had gone for my ankle. 'You will tell me all those secrets, little girl,' he said, imitating a scene from the movie. 'Or else we will have to k-e-e-l-l you in a very nasty way . . .'

'Yeah,' said Cat with a nod at the sofa. 'Get your weapons ready.'

That's the trouble with getting in with a crowd like this, who have all known each other for a while. There's telepathy between them and with just a nod, they all know what the others are thinking. They each picked up a cushion from the back of the sofa and held them up ready to bash me.

'You're all mad,' I said. 'And ganging up on me isn't going to make me tell you anything.'

'Ah. So there *is* something,' said Squidge, lifting his cushion up in readiness.

'No, I didn't say that.'

'You did,' Squidge insisted. 'Didn't she, guys?'

The others nodded and moved a bit closer in on me.

'OK. OK. There might be something but it's nothing bad.'

'I *knew* it,' said Squidge. 'Tell us or you're a dead man . . . woman . . . girl . . . gerbil . . .'

I shook my head. Squidge gave the others a nod and they all pounced at once. In a second, I'd been wrestled to the floor and was being smothered with cushions. I wriggled free, grabbed my own cushion and began to defend myself.

'Ai ya!' I cried as I stood up and went into my best ninja warrior pose. 'Do not come near me as I am a yellow belt.'

Mac went into kung fu stance opposite me. 'And I am a brown belt.'

Becca and Cat got up to join in. 'And we are . . . what are we?' asked Cat.

'Green belts,' said Becca, then laughed. 'Or does that mean something else?'

'Forget that,' said Squidge as he made a dash for my legs. 'I know how to get her to talk. Get her feet. Tickle her feet. She can't stand it.'

Once again they pounced and no way could I fend the four of them off. Cat, Becca and Squidge pinned me down while Mac pulled my socks off and began to tickle my feet. It was excruciating.

'Arrrrghhhhhh, g-e-e-e-e-e-e-t o-o-o-o-o-o-f-f-f-f-f-f,' I wailed as I began to laugh and scream at the same time.

Seconds later, the door opened and Dad appeared.

'Hey, what's all the racket?' he asked as he took in the scattered cushions, spilt crisps and writhing bodies on the floor in front of him. 'It sounds like someone is being murdered.'

Squidge and Mac immediately released me and sat back on their heels looking embarrassed. Becca looked out of the window as if she'd seen something fascinating and Cat tried to look invisible.

'Er, nothing, Dad. We were just messing about,' I said.

'Then can you do it a bit more quietly?' he asked. 'From out there in the kitchen, you sound like a bunch of rioting football fans whose team have just lost. And Mac and Squidge, you should be an example to the others seeing as you're both sixteen.'

'Yes, Mr Axford,' said Squidge.

'Sorry, Mr Axford,' said Mac.

Dad rolled his eyes. 'Call me Zac. Mr Axford makes me sound ancient.'

I got the giggles then as they all looked so sheepish. Sometimes I think my friends are intimidated by my dad and not because he's at all frightening or strict or scary. He's actually really gentle. I think it's because he's so famous.

'And what's so funny, Lia?' asked Dad. 'And why are there crisps all over the rug?'

'Squidge thinks that I'm not telling him something,' I said, knowing that he'd understand my dilemma. 'And he decided to beat the information out of me.'

Dad turned to look at Squidge who by now looked like he wanted the rug to open up and swallow him. 'Oh he did, did he?'

'Not seriously. I wouldn't hurt her,' Squidge blurted.

'And is this how you treat all the girls in your life who choose not to tell you something?' Dad teased, causing Squidge to squirm and join Mac in blushing furiously.

'Er . . . no, I . . . course not . . .' he stuttered.

Dad turned to me. 'And did you tell him what he wanted to know?'

'No way,' I said and zipped my lips.

Dad winked at me. 'Good girl.' Then he turned to the others. 'Don't worry. You'll find out the news soon enough.'

And with that, he went out of the room.

'So there *is* something,' said Squidge. 'Why can't you tell us?'

'Because I promised Dad,' I said. 'It's a secret.'

'Is your mum pregnant?' asked Cat.

'Ewww,' I said. 'Don't even go there. But no, that's not it.'

Squidge looked worried. 'Hey. You're not moving, are you?'

I took his hand and gave it a squeeze. 'No. We're not moving.'

'You're changing schools again?' he asked.

I shook my head again.

'Divorce,' said Mac. 'Your mum's having an affair with the milkman.'

'Nooo,' I said.

'Your dad's having an affair with the milkman?' asked Squidge.

'*Noooo*,' I said, laughing. 'And I'm not telling you. Now let's change the subject.'

'Yeah,' said Cat. 'Give her a break. If she doesn't want to tell, she doesn't want to tell. Now I wanted to check you all out for something. Weekend after next, it's the summer fête at the vicar's house in Cawsand. I know, I know. . . *boring*, but it could be a laugh if we're all there. Dad's roped me in to sell cakes baked by the local ladies but will the rest of you come?'

'Sure,' said Squidge and Becca.

'Not sure,' said Mac. 'Have to see what the guest situation is.' Mac's mum runs an upmarket B&B and often has guests at the weekends now that the weather is getting better. She likes Mac to be around to run errands and help out as he is the only man in their house since she divorced Mac's dad.

'Lia?' asked Cat.

'Er . . .' I couldn't say without spilling the beans. That was the weekend Dad had pencilled in for his surprise. 'Might be busy.'

'Doing what?' asked Squidge.

'Can't say.'

Squidge went to mock strangle me and just as he had his hands around my throat, Dad walked in again and caught him. He gave Squidge a quizzical look as he searched for his glasses and Squidge whipped his hands away and sat on them looking sheepish again. I couldn't stop laughing.

After Dad had gone again, Squidge sighed heavily. 'He's going to think that I'm a total axe murderer,' he said, then his face brightened. 'I know how we'll get it out of you without strangulation, Lia. Truth, dare, kiss or promise.'

'Oh no,' said Mac. 'Not that again. I thought we were finished with that.'

'Yeah,' said Becca. 'It leads to all sorts of trouble.' Then she grinned. 'So no options, just the truth, Lia. You have to tell us the truth.' She began to count off her fingers. 'Clue one. There is a mystery. Clue two. Something is going on that you can't tell us but your dad's in on it. Clue three. It is possibly going to take place the weekend after next. Hhhmmmm? I *know*. Easy. Your mum's having one of her parties. That's it, isn't it? She's Gemini. Her birthday is in

June. I remember. Can we come? I love your mum's parties.'

It wasn't a bad guess from Becca as usually my mum likes nothing better than to throw a party. The bigger the better. Christmas. Birthdays. Valentine's. Any excuse. All sorts of themes and no money spared. And it was coming up to her birthday. Her fortieth birthday. But she'd been acting really weird about it saying that she wanted no fuss. No big do. 'Mid-life crisis,' Ollie had said by way of explanation. All of us tried our best to talk her into doing something but she was adamant that she just wanted to 'get it over with in as quiet manner as possible'.

As the time got closer, Dad began to panic. 'It's not right. I know women. I know your mother. She may be saying forget it but when it comes to the day, she'll want the works. We'd better organise something and we'd better organise it quick!'

Loads of ideas flew about. Weekend at a spa. Gorgeous piece of jewellery. Watch. New car. Clothes. But she had all that.

In the end, the plan that appealed the most was to book a small hotel somewhere fabulous and then invite a bunch of her friends to go and stay there as Dad's guests. And I was going to be allowed to invite my friends, all expenses paid. Mum wouldn't know anything about it. Dad would say that he'd honoured her request to do something small and that he was taking her away, just the two of them. She'd never guess and then taraaah! When she got to the hotel, there would be her family and some friends waiting.

That was the secret but seeing as it was all decided at the last minute, Dad wanted to be sure of the flights and the hotel rooms before I was allowed to mention it to Cat, Becca, Mac and Squidge. He'd been researching all sorts of locations but some of them didn't have the space for so many people at such short notice. I was dying to tell the others but he'd made me swear that I wouldn't until it was definite as he didn't want anybody getting all excited then being let down, plus he didn't want the secret leaking out and getting back to Mum. I couldn't wait to tell them all. A couple of days in a fab location not only with my friends but with Squidge. My lovely gorgeous Squidge. I'd be sure to get him alone then. It was going to be so fantastic. And so romantic.

'So is it a party?' Becca asked again.

'Might be, might not be,' I said. 'I will tell you as soon as I can. The whole truth and nothing but the truth so help me. But not yet. You have to give me another couple of days.'

'Pff,' said Cat. 'I hate secrets. My imagination goes into overdrive.'

'Mine too,' said Becca. 'But I don't think she's going to tell us.'

Mac flicked 'play' on the remote and we went back to watching the teen heroes on the screen get their heads ripped off. At least Squidge put his arm round me and cuddled me up to him.

After the movie was over, he stayed behind for a while and at last we got our snogging session in.

'And don't think I'm going to give in and tell you everything just because you're a great kisser,' I said as we pulled back to get our breath.

'Aw,' he groaned. 'I was hoping my change of tactic might work.'

I was about to explain again that I couldn't tell when he shook his head. 'Only teasing,' he said. 'You tell in your own time. Just one thing. The truth, dare, kiss, promise thing. It is important, yeah? I know you need a few days before you can tell your Dad's secret, but with us, between us. Truth. It's important yeah?'

I nodded. 'Yeah.'

'So let's pledge to always tell each other the truth. Even if it hurts.'

'Yeah. Definitely,' I said. 'But I'd never have anything to say to hurt you.'

'I hope not,' said Squidge and put his deep zombie voice on again. 'Because then I really would have to k-e-e-e-l-l-l-l you.'

Bag or Babe?

'SEEN DAD?' I ASKED MUM after Squidge had left later that same day.

Mum pointed out of the kitchen window to Dad's music studio down by the lake behind the stables. 'Down there, I think.'

'Thanks,' I said and headed for the back door.

'Are you two up to something?' asked Mum.

'Me? Dad?' I replied, putting on my best innocent face. 'Like what?'

'Like organising a surprise party for me,' said Mum. 'I told you, I don't want one.'

I went and sat at the breakfast bar where she was busy grinding seeds with a pestle and mortar. Behind her at another counter, our housekeeper Meena was preparing vegetables for supper.

'What are you making?' I asked.

'I'm grinding coriander and fennel seeds to put in a marinade,' she replied. 'Meena's doing sweet potato. And don't change the subject.'

I laughed. 'I wasn't. Just there's nothing to say. Dad and I aren't up to anything and we've got the message loud and clear that you don't want a party.'

'That's OK, then. So why do you want your dad?'

'Oh . . . homework thing,' I lied.

'I can help with homework.'

'Maths thing. He's better than you are.'

'No, he's not. He's rubbish at accounts. You are up to something, aren't you?'

Is everyone in my life a mind-reader? I asked myself as I looked at the floor in case, like Squidge, she could read my thoughts.

'Why don't you want to celebrate, Mum?' I asked. 'Normally you do.'

'Well, for one thing, we're already having a party for midsummer towards the end of June. Seems a bit mad to have one so close to the other.'

'But the midsummer night party is for one of your charities. This one would be for you. To celebrate.'

'What? Being forty. What's to celebrate?'

'But you look brilliant for your age.'

This time I wasn't lying. I knew I had the best-looking mum in the area. She has great cheekbones and flawless skin, hair like silk cut to her shoulders and even without make-up she still looks beautiful.

'Brilliant "for my age",' said Mum. 'Poo to that.' She stopped grinding the seeds for a moment. 'I don't really know why I don't want a party. I just don't. I want to forget all about it. It's strange, being forty. I don't feel it. I feel like I'm eighteen inside and then I look in the mirror and see this old face looking back at me . . .'

'Rubbish. You haven't got an old face . . .'

'Yes, I have, and it's going to get even older. Forty. Forty-five, fifty . . .'

'But they say life begins at forty,' I said.

Mum smiled. 'Yeah. Maybe. Yeah. Maybe it will begin but it doesn't mean that I have to announce to the whole world I am now middle-aged.'

'Never. You don't look it,' I said. 'And anyway, being middle-aged is a state of mind.'

Mum laughed again. 'A state of mind! Where did you hear that?'

'I read it in one of your magazines,' I said. 'And I think they're right. You have a choice at any age. Look like a bag or a babe. The choice is yours. And you look like a babe. With all your fresh juices and organic food, your skin looks great. You exercise. You look after yourself. I think you look about twenty-eight.'

Mum came round the bar and kissed me lightly on the top of my head. 'Dear Lia. You say all the right things.'

I smiled back at her and got up to go to the back door again as she went back to her preparations for supper.

'But still no surprises,' she said as my hand reached for the door.

'I'm not sure this is a good idea any more,' I said when I found Dad five minutes later. He was in his studio with our two red setters, Max and Molly, who were sleeping under his desk. 'Mum's really not into having anything.'

'But what's the alternative?' asked Dad. 'We do as she asks and then on the day, she'll feel let down. No. I know women and I know your mum. I learned very very early on. Our first Valentine's Day. Oh, she said, don't get me anything, it's such a commercial venture. The only people that really benefit are the businessmen behind the cards and merchandise. I took her at her word. No card. No present. She sulked all day. It was only when I went and bought her some flowers and a red chocolate heart that she smiled again. So now I know that when she says, "I don't want a fuss", she really means, "I want the biggest, almightiest most fantastic fuss in the history of mankind".'

I laughed. He might be right. I remember when Squidge turned sixteen just before Easter, he said the same thing to his parents. Oh, don't make a fuss (although in his case it was because he knew that they didn't have any extra money). But they threw him a surprise party and spoiled him and he was really blown away. He told me afterwards that before the party, when he'd thought that everyone had taken him at his word, he'd felt disappointed and unloved. I don't want Mum feeling that way. Not for a moment.

'I think you're right, Dad. People say the opposite of what they mean sometimes. And forty is a big one, isn't it?'

'Sixteen. Twenty-one. Thirty. Forty. Fifty. All biggies. New chapters. And to be celebrated, I say. Like – you've got this far. And here are all the people who are happy about that fact to help you make a day of it.'

'So what have we got so far?' I asked.

Dad opened his palms to indicate all the brochures on the desk in front of him. Venice, Florence, Paris, Rome, Italian lakes, South of France, Scotland.

'Susie's on the case up in London but we have to narrow it down a bit I reckon,' he said. (Susie is Dad's PA and is absolutely brilliant. She does all his tour arrangements, books hotels, flights and so on.)

I picked up a couple of the brochures and flopped down on the sofa by the bay window. 'So where? America? Florida? We had a good time there a couple of years ago, didn't we? Or maybe we should go back to New York?'

'Too many relatives I think she'd rather avoid over there,' said Dad with a grimace. 'No. I envisage somewhere more exotic.'

I flicked through a brochure showing turquoise seas and clear blue skies. 'The Far East?'

Dad got up from his desk and went to the big American fridge in the corner of the room. 'Might be a bit too far for some people. Can take eleven hours to get to some of the locations. Juice?'

'Yeah, thanks. So where?'

Dad took a couple of small cartons of juice out and chucked one over to me. 'We've left it a bit late, so it might be wherever they can have us all at such short notice. Susie's checking out availability.'

'How many of us are there so far?'

Dad glanced down at his list. 'About twenty-five. Five of

you lot,' he said, 'that is if Mac, Squidge, Cat and Becca all come . . .'

'I'm sure they will when they hear but I think we'll need to tell them soon. Cat is already making plans and roping in the others for that weekend in June. It's the village fête in Cawsand.'

Dad stroked his chin. 'Is it? Right. Yes. OK. Let them know what's happening but swear them to secrecy. I don't want your mum overhearing the whole plan while she's in the village.'

'Right. So who else?'

Dad looked back at his list. 'Star of course. She's bringing her friends Rhiannon and George.'

Brilliant, I thought. I liked both of them and so did Mum. Rhiannon was Star's oldest mate and was like one of the family and George was a stylist who worked on a lot of Star's photo shoots. He was a hoot. Star always said he was the perfect man, so it was a shame for her that he was gay.

'Grandma and Grandpa Newman have opted out. They're not too keen on flying anymore. Grandma Axford will be coming depending on the location. Says she's not going anywhere she has to have injections for. Your Aunt Cydney will be joining us and then about ten close friends and whoever Ollie brings.'

'And who does Ollie want to bring?'

'So far, he's mentioned Henry Lynch, Jamie Parker and Michael Bradley.'

I almost spat my drink out. 'Michael Bradley? Why does Ollie have to bring *him*?'

'Because he's been his best friend since forever, you know that. Why? Is it a problem?'

'Oh no, not really,' I blustered, trying to recover as fast as I could. Michael Bradley! Finking stinking. He was only the boy I'd had a crush on since I was out of nappies but he'd never taken much notice of me. At least not as a girl. I was always Ollie's kid sister. Little Lia. Last year, he came down with Ollie and I got all excited (this was before Squidge) and imagined that at last he might notice that I had grown up. And he did, I think. For a moment I thought that all my fantasies were about to come true and then who appeared next to him but his girlfriend Usha. She's a stunning Indian girl, and as far as I knew, they were still an item.

'But won't Michael want to bring Usha?' I asked.

Dad shook his head. 'Not necessarily. The party is for your mum, not for Ollie. We can't take everyone, and anyway, it's only for a long weekend. If we invited everyone, we'd have a list a mile long.'

'Why doesn't Ollie bring one of his many girlfriends instead of Michael?' I asked.

'I doubt if Cat would enjoy the trip very much if he did,' said Dad and then smiled. 'No need to look at me like that. I know what goes on. And I know Ollie likes to see Cat when he's down here.'

'I think they've cooled it lately,' I said. I didn't fill Dad in on all the details but at the beginning of May, Ollie met a girl up in London who came down here in the last half-term holidays. I don't think he could decide between her and Cat and was spinning them both along in the hope that he could get away with it. Sadly for him, his plan backfired but that's another story.

'Oh, why's that?' asked Dad.

I shrugged. 'You know Ollie. Commitment phobic. Don't think he knows what he wants. But anyway, I still don't see why he has to bring Michael . . .'

'Has something happened between you and Michael that you're not telling me about?' asked Dad. 'Has he done something to upset you?'

'No. No. Not really.'

Dad was staring at me. Arrghhh, I thought, *another* person trying to do the mind-reading thing!

'Come on, spill,' said Dad.

'Nothing to spill,' I said.

Dad laughed. 'Known you too long. And you're a lousy liar.'

'That's what Squidge said.'

'Squidge is right. So has this Michael done something to upset you? Don't worry. If you don't want to tell me, I'll just let Ollie know that Michael can't come on the trip.'

'Oh God *nooooo*,' I blurted. 'Don't do that.' That would make an issue of it and then Ollie would be on my case and he was one person I *really* didn't want to know about my crush.

I decided to tell Dad as I knew he could be trusted. 'OK. Just between us. No biggie. School crush way back. Temporary moment of insanity although he is major cute. But no. I'm sooooo over it. Let Michael come and pleeeeeeeese never ever, ever, ever mention this to Ollie. Ever. It will be fine. I'll be fine. I'm with Squidge now and anyway Michael is still with Usha.'

Dad smiled. 'I won't say anything. First love, huh . . .?'

'Yeah. Mad, really.'

Dad looked thoughtful for a moment. 'Actually, I could see you and Michael together. He's a nice lad. Yeah. Want me to arrange a marriage when you're older?'

'Daadd!'

'Only joking. But I do like Michael. A bright boy.'

'I think we should change the subject like *right* now! Who was your first love?' I asked.

'Proper?'

I nodded.

'Your mum. Really. I had girlfriends before. Girls I liked, even thought I loved – but then . . . I still remember that first time I saw your mother. She knocked me out.'

I'd heard the story a million times and still loved hearing it. Dad's face always lit up when he told it. 'Where was it?'

Dad slapped his forehead. 'Of course, that's it. That's where we should go . . .'

'What? Where?'

'Morocco! Obvious. The first time I saw your mother. She was on holiday with her mother and staying in a converted palace in the medina in Marrakech. Way out of my league back then. Things were only just starting to happen for me. I was a nobody. A musician. Broke and bumming it with my mate Barry. As sheer cheek, Barry and I decided to go and have a beer in the posh joint with our last few coins. We were at the bar and your mum walked in. Pure class. All dressed in white. Grace Kelly all over again.'

'Grace Kelly?'

Dad grinned. 'Big-time movie star. Became princess of Monaco and died tragically in a car accident . . .'

'Oh, I know,' I said. 'I think I've seen pictures of her family in *Hello!* magazine. Princess Caroline of Monaco. She's her daughter, right?'

Dad nodded. 'That's right. But *yes*, Morocco. Why didn't I think of this before? It will be perfect. The weather will be lovely at this time of year. It's only three hours or so on the plane. And . . . yeah! I wonder if I could get the place where she stayed. Where we met. What do you think?'

'Excellent plan. That would be brilliant. I think that's a great idea, Dad,' I said, then smiled at him. 'You're almost as romantic as Squidge.'

But Dad didn't hear the last bit. He'd already picked up the phone and was asking Susie to check out details for the hotel in Marrakech.

'Want to have a look?' he asked a few minutes later when he'd finished his call. 'I can find the hotel on the Net. Riad Rhoul, it's not the biggest but it is one of the best.'

He punched in a few buttons on his keyboard and before long a site came up.

'Wow,' I said as the photo gallery downloaded and the most fabulously exotic pictures appeared on the screen. Tiled fountains set among tropical flowers and trees. A turquoise pool surrounded by shrubs and sun loungers. Little alcoves with cushioned seats set against mosaic walls. Gorgeous balconies where muslin curtains wafted in a breeze. Coloured lanterns hanging over terraces. And the bedrooms looked like something out of *Tales of the Arabian Nights*. Deep red walls, silken beds with golden pillows.

'She's going to love this,' said Dad as his phone rang. 'I don't know why I didn't think of it before.' He picked up and listened to whoever was on the other end of the line.

When he put down the phone, he gave me the thumbs up then grinned widely. 'Susie's on the case and I think we might be in business. She's found it. Apparently it's used mainly for occasions like this now. Private parties. Weddings, birthdays and so on but it might be free at least for one or two nights the weekend we want. Fingers crossed. Susie's looked on the Net and it all looks OK but she needs to call the offices in the morning when they are open. So I think it's time to let your pals know that they can earmark the date.'

Morocco. Marrakech. Squidge was going to love it.

3 Finking Stinking

I RACED BACK UP TO THE HOUSE and up to my room where I could make my calls in private. Of course I wanted to tell Squidge the news first but he wasn't at home and his stupid mobile was on answer. Grrrrrr. Finking stinking frustrating. I felt so excited I would burst if I didn't tell someone soon.

I left him a message to call me *urgently*.

Oh, where was he? I wondered. I wanted to hear his reaction as I knew he'd be over the moon and a trip away is just what we needed at this stage of our relationship. I'd been feeling lately that I needed something to keep Squidge interested in me. He doesn't know it but loads of girls at school and in the area fancy him and not just because he's cute looking but because he's the most brilliant company. Full of life and excited about what he's just read or seen or wants to do. We'd been going out together for a couple of months, since before Easter, and part of me was worried that Squidge might get bored once he found out how ordinary I was. I wished I had a unique talent that he could admire – like Mac, for instance. He's the most brill cartoonist, and he and Squidge talk art for hours. And Becca, she has a stunning voice and also writes her own songs (which aren't so great) but she and Squidge love to discuss the latest music and CDs in the lunch breaks at school. And Cat is brilliant and warm and funny and strong. She and Squidge have known each other since forever. They gas for hours about all the local gossip and what's going on in the village. And then there's Squidge himself. He's a one off. His photographs are really good and so are the films he makes on his digital camera. He wants to be either a film director or photographer when he's finished school.

I wish I had something like that. A talent. A goal. Or I wish I was one of those people who could make everyone laugh all the time. Or come out with brilliant opinions that would make everyone think. But I don't. I watch. I listen. I know that my family is different and *that's* interesting in the beginning. But what was there to keep Squidge interested in me once the novelty of dating an Axford wore off? So, a trip away somewhere would be stunning. Not every girl could offer him that.

I couldn't wait for Squidge to call back. I phoned him again and left a message on his voice mail.

'OK. So this is the secret. Dad wants to invite you to come to Morocco with us the weekend after next to celebrate Mum's fortieth. To Marrakech if we can get the rooms and flights. You can't tell anyone in case Mum finds out. All expenses paid by Dad so it won't cost anything. All you have to do is ask your parents and then swear them to secrecy. Call me as *soon* as you get this.'

Next was Cat. She let out a low whistle. 'Me? Honest? Wow. Ohmigod. *Ohmigod*. I hope Dad lets me go. Oh please oh please oh please . . . I'll go and ask him right now. I'll call you back. Ohmigod. The furthest away I've ever been is London. So Morocco. Wow! OK. Going now. Call you back.'

After Cat, I called Becca who was equally blown out.

'*Yaaaaaaaay*,' she squealed down the phone. 'I knew it. I *knew* it. I knew it was something to do with your mum's birthday. Call you straight back. I'll just go and ask Mum and Dad but I'm sure it will be fine. And if it isn't, I'll run away and join you as no way am I missing this.'

And Mac was fourth.

'Morocco? You're kidding? Like, *yeah*,' he said. 'One hundred million per cent count me in.'

And then I had to sit and twiddle my thumbs while I waited for them all to call back to confirm. I crept downstairs, checked that Mum was settled in the red room watching telly then I tiptoed along the wooden floor in the corridor to the library and looked for the travel section. There were books there from all over the world. Arabella, the interior designer Mum used when we first bought the house, had done a great job. It was just like a proper library with separate sections: reference, fiction, health, history, food, gardening, travel and so on. Arabella came down from London twice a year to update it.

I glanced over the shelves until I found the travel books for M. Malaysia, Mombasa, Morocco. I pulled out the book, found the chapters on Marrakech and sat in one of the chairs by the fireplace to read. It looked amazing. A walled city set against the Atlas mountains. And it looked like the weather would be hot hot hot.

After a few moments, the house phone flashed that there was a call. I leapt up and grabbed it before anyone else could answer.

It was Mac.

'Hey, Lia,' he said and I could tell from those two words that it was going to be bad news. 'I can't go.'

'But why not? It won't cost anything.'

'Four little letters,' he said. 'GCSE. Mum hit the roof when I suggested Morocco and said absolutely no way and that I'd had too much time off recently anyway. It's sucks.'

'Did you tell her that you'd study while you were away?'

'I did and she laughed. Said she's been to Morocco and no way would I get a minute's studying done, too many things to see. It's rotten, isn't it?'

'Yes,' I agreed. 'Rotten.' In the excitement of the moment, I'd forgotten that the boys would be doing their exams in a few weeks. Part of me understood Mac's mum's reaction. I'm sure if I suggested a few days away to my parents before some of the most important exams in the school calendar, they'd say no way too. I felt my heart sink. Squidge's parents would be bound to say the same thing.

'Have you heard from the others yet?' asked Mac.

'Not yet. I haven't even been able to get hold of Squidge but I reckon his mum and dad will say the same as yours.'

'Yeah. Exams. Bummer.'

'Yeah. Major bummer. There's always the party on midsummer night though. You can come to that still.'

'Yeah. And that reminds me. We're doing *A Midsummer*

Night's Dream for GCSE,' said Mac. 'Better do some more revision on it.'

He didn't sound excited about the party at all.

After I'd put the phone down, I closed the book on Marrakech and just as I was about to put it back on the shelf, Mum came in.

'Who was on the phone?'

'Mac.'

'What did he want?'

'Nothing.'

'Nothing, huh? And what are you doing in here?' she said as she spied the book. 'Travel books. What are you looking at them for?'

'School project.'

'On Morocco?'

'No. No . . . that one fell out. No, on Malaysia,' I said in the hope that I could put her off the scent.

I was about to pull out the book on Malaysia and get her looking at that when the phone went again. Mum picked it up and then held it out for me.

'Becca.'

I took the phone and tried to will Mum out of the room but it didn't look as though she was in any hurry to go anywhere.

'I'm in,' said an excited voice at the other end. 'When are we leaving? What airport? My mum wants to talk to your dad and of course they have to OK it with the school. What time do we get back? Where are we staying? What are you taking? What will the weather be like? How many days do we need to take off school? Do you think Mrs Jeffries will let us?'

I wanted to laugh at Becca's breathless questions but I swear Mum was trying to listen in as she was hovering behind me pretending to be looking at some books.

'Yes,' I said. 'You left it here . . .'

'Uh? Left what?'

'I'll bring it into school tomorrow. Don't worry. I won't forget.'

'Ah, you can't talk?' asked Becca as the penny dropped at her end.

'Exactly,' I said with a sigh of relief.

'Your mum still there?'

'Looks like it,' I said as casually as I could.

'Speak later. I'll ring your mobile so she can't eavesdrop. Your room.'

'Later,' I said and hung up.

'And what did Becca want?' asked Mum.

'Left a book here.'

Mum nodded but she looked like she didn't believe a word of it.

And then the phone went *again*. Once more, Mum picked up.

'Cat,' she said as she held out the phone. 'You girls have only just seen each other this afternoon when you all piled over after school. What is going on?'

'Nothing.' I shrugged and took the phone from her.

'Hi, Cat.'

'Your mum's there, isn't she?'

'Yep.'

'OK. I'll talk, you listen.'

'Yep.'

'I can come.'

'YEP!' I glanced over at Mum to see if she was still listening in but she seemed to have lost interest and a moment later she left the room. I sighed with relief.

'Phew. She's gone. Oh Cat, I'm soooooo pleased. Bec can too. So we'll all be together. Us girls. Oh, but Mac can't come. GCSEs. His mum said no way.'

'I thought that might happen and he has been up to London a lot lately staying with his dad. His mum has been on his case ever since. What about Squidge? Have you heard from him?'

'Not yet but after Mac, I'm not holding out too much hope. It will be so rotten if he can't come. I mean, don't get me wrong, I'm so pleased you're coming but can you imagine, a few days in the most fab of fab places with my boyfriend.'

'Yes. It would be fantastic. So . . . Er . . . will Ollie be going?' asked Cat.

'Yeah. Course. But I thought that you weren't interested in him any more?'

'I am and I'm not,' said Cat. 'I know what he's like but hey, a weekend away. Could be fun. I have no expectations from him. Like, no strings, etc. Shame if Squidge won't be able to go though. Will Ollie be bringing any of his mates?'

'Yes. Ohmigod . . . He will. And what if Squidge isn't there . . .?'

'What do you mean?'

'Dad said Ollie could bring three of his mates.'

'Well that will be brill, won't it? Bec will be well pleased. Some new boys to flirt with. I can hang out with Ollie. It will be a laugh.'

'Ollie's mates are Henry Lynch, Jamie Parker and Michael Bradley.'

'Michael Bradley?' Cat repeated. 'Oh! Isn't he the one . . .?'

'Yep. Exactly. The one I had a major crush on.'

'But that was ages ago . . .'

'Yeah. But still. I don't know what it'll be like, being locked up with him in some seven-star hotel . . .'

'Seven-star? I didn't think there were seven-star hotels . . .'

'I mean, posh and a half. Oh Cat . . . I thought it would be OK because Squidge would be coming and I'd be with him and now maybe he won't be . . .'

'Haven't the London boys got exams too?'

'Lower Sixth, so nothing too major and Ollie wouldn't miss this. Not for anything.'

'Do you think you would be tempted by Michael?'

If Cat had been in the room, she would have seen me blush. Michael was the star of every snogging fantasy I had until I met Squidge and even though I was dating Squidge and would never be unfaithful, I couldn't deny something that had been such a big part of my life (even if it was my fantasy life).

'No. No way. I would never be unfaithful to Squidge. Anyway, Michael's with someone too. Remember Usha, the girl he brought down with him last time he was down?'

'Oh yeah,' said Cat.

'It will be fine. Better if he wasn't coming but who can say? I haven't spent any time with him for ages and I'm sure all those old feelings will have gone. I mean, so much has happened since then. Like Squidge. He's all I want.'

'Hey, it will be OK,' said Cat. 'Whatever happens. We'll look after you.'

After I'd put the phone down, I thought about Cat's question. Would I be tempted? *Would* I? I'd been in love with Michael ever since I could remember so why would that suddenly change? He was really gorgeous and clever and funny. All the things I liked in a boy. But Squidge was all those things too. It would be OK.

Squidge, Squidge, Squidge.

I needn't have worried. The next call to come through was from the man himself.

He began singing a song that I'd heard Dad play from the Sixties about 'boarding the Marrakech Express'.

'Got your message and it's a goer,' said Squidge.

'Really? You've asked your parents and everything?' I asked.

'Yepideedoodah, yepideeday. They're totally cool.'

'But how? Mac's mum said no because of his exams . . .'

'Really? He must be well bummed out.'

'I thought yours would be the same.'

'Ah yes, but part of my coursework is taking photos. I

talked mine round by convincing them that there is no better place on the planet to take fab photos than Marrakech. And it's true. They'll be such a fantastic contrast to my pics of grey skies and windy beaches down here. All those wonderful Moroccan colours, ochres, reds, yellows. The Atlas mountains. The souks. The medinas. New pics will really help my portfolio when I apply for art college.'

'Good thinking, Batman,' I said. 'Well done. Shame Mac couldn't take a similar line with his parents.'

'Yeah. He must be so pissed off. We'll have to do something to cheer him up when we get back. Or maybe we should bring something fab back for him. Like his very own dancing girl. Wow, Lia. It's going to be great. Apparently the light in northern Africa is amazing. I can't wait. I really will be able to get some brilliant shots. Sunrises. Sunsets. Great locations. Portraits of you. You must say a humungous thanks to your dad. This is so ace. The best thing that's ever happened to me after meeting you.'

He sounded so happy. We'd have the time of our lives.

Michael Bradley wasn't going to be a problem at all.

Teen Truants

'Noooooo,' I groaned. 'She can't have.'

'She can and she has,' said Dad. 'She won't allow it.'

I'd just got home from school on Wednesday and Dad beckoned me to join him in the red room where he quickly closed the door behind me.

'So what did she say?'

By she, I meant Mrs Peterson, my headmistress. Dad had been talking to her that afternoon to check that it was OK for Cat, Becca, Squidge and me to leave school early on the Friday of Mum's birthday. 'Early' meaning 'probably not go in at all that day'.

'Do you realise, Mr Axford, that unauthorised absences count as truancy when the inspectors come in?' said Dad in a high female-sounding voice.

He was as far from how Mrs Peterson actually sounded as he could possibly be and I almost laughed but I was too worried that we might not be able to go to Morocco after all.

'But we can't *not* go now. You've booked the hotel and everything.'

Dad sank back on the sofa and was swiftly joined by Max and Molly, one on either side of him. 'I know. I know. Maybe it was a bad idea in the first place. This sort of thing ought to have been organised months ahead. My fault. I should have done it sooner.'

'We can say we were all ill,' I suggested.

'And you don't think that Mrs Peterson would put two and two together? Bit of a coincidence, all of you just happening to fall ill on the day that we fly off to Morocco.'

'Could happen. We're all mates. We could all eat the same batch of prawns or some seafood . . . food poisoning. Happens all the time.'

'No, Lia.'

'Oh, let's just go. It's only a day . . .'

'*No*, Lia. You know how I feel about these things. I don't want anyone thinking that there's one set of rules for the general public and another for the Axfords who make up their own. *I especially* don't want your teachers thinking that.'

I felt my stomach start to churn. Now I could understand why he hadn't wanted to tell people about the trip until it was all definite. To set something up and imagine yourself there only to be told later that it's a no go was too painful.

'What about Ollie? Have you spoken to his headmaster?'

Dad nodded. 'I spoke to Dr Howard just before Mrs Peterson. As luck would have it, the timing couldn't be more perfect because that Friday is an in-service training day at his school – all the staff have to go, something about health and safety – so the pupils have the day off and Ollie was going to come down here for a long weekend.'

'But . . . you can't leave me here and all go and . . .'

Dad reached over and put his hand on mine. 'We're not going to leave you, Lia. We wouldn't do that. Just maybe rethink the plan. Something simpler as there have been a couple of problems. Your school isn't the only one. Susie's been on the phone all day. The hotel is confirmed so that's sorted; it's just getting everyone there that might be tricky. She's got the flight booked for your mother and me, but to get everyone else over will mean people travelling on two, maybe three separate flights. I was hoping to get everyone on together.'

'We'll be OK,' I said. 'I'll be with Star and Ollie and Cat and Becca and Squidge. When are the flights?'

'Some on the Thursday, some on the Friday but as I said, you can't get out of school . . .'

'But, Dad, everyone does it all the time.'

'No, Lia. We play by the rules. OK, so everyone does it but their names don't end up plastered all over the front page of the newspapers if they step out of line, do they? Can you imagine? It only takes one person to leak the story. Teens play truant thanks to Zac Axford, irresponsible, etc, etc.'

Suddenly I understood. Dad may have been at his peak in the Eighties but that didn't mean that the press had lost interest. They still hounded him when there was the slightest whiff of a story. Last year, Dad had been up in London and met with my Aunt Cydney for lunch. Mum was held up somewhere so it was just Dad and Cydney. Next day, it was all over the tabloids. Photos of them in a little tête-a-tête with the headline: *Zac Axford ditches wife for a lookalike younger model.* Mum and Cydney thought it was hysterical but Dad wasn't amused. 'Stories like that can put a strain on the happiest of families,' he said. 'People always come out with the "no smoke without fire" line and no matter what you say in your own defence, you sound guilty.' From almost as soon as I could walk and talk, I'd been taught to toe the line and never do anything that could be misconstrued by the press. Not that they were interested in me but I understood why Dad didn't want to pull the three of us out of school and say, 'Oh to hell with it.'

'So what are you going to do?' I asked.

Dad shook his head. 'Don't know yet. And before you ask, we've already checked flights for the Saturday. There's one seat on one plane but there's no way you're travelling alone and anyway, you'd hardly get to spend any time there and you'd miss the dinner on Friday night. We've tried all the airlines. It seems there's some sort of convention happening on the Sunday. I don't know; maybe it's not meant to be. But what else can I do? Arrange a big picnic in Mount Edgcumbe park? I don't know. I've blown it. Left it too late.'

I shook my head. 'Picnic? Doesn't sound the same, does it? So should I let the others know?'

'Not yet,' said Dad as he turned to the window and gazed out. 'Look, leave it with me.'

He looked so sad. Even Max and Molly sensed that something was wrong and looked at him with concern.

'You can't give up, Dad,' I said. 'There has to be a solution.'

'Like what? I'm a rock star, not a magician.'

And that's when I had my idea.

'Yes, Dad. That's it. You're a rock star. You *are* a rock star. So maybe it's time to act like one.'

Dad looked puzzled. 'What do you mean?'

'Spend a bit of your dosh. It's Mum's birthday. Splash out.'

'I'm going to. That hotel isn't cheap, believe me . . .'

'I'm sure it isn't,' I said. 'How much have you got in the bank?'

'Dunno. My accountant does all that.'

'Roughly?'

'Couple of mill . . .'

'Couple of million?'

'Yeah. Couple of million comes in every year. Used to be more.'

'Every year? Then for heaven's sake, Dad. Isn't it obvious?'

'I'm not with you, love. Isn't what obvious?'

I spread my arms out to look like wings and play-acted flying round the room.

'Lia, what on earth are you doing?'

'The solution, Dad. Simple. No flights on commercial airlines. I bet that doesn't stop Elton John or Paul McCartney or Mick Jagger.'

Dad was still looking at me as though I was mad.

'Hire . . . a . . . plane . . .'

Itinerary

SUSIE WORKED MIRACLES and soon it was sorted. Mum and Dad were booked first class on a commercial airline on Friday morning. And not one but *two* private planes for the guests! One to leave from London early afternoon for those who lived near there. And one for the Cornish contingent who were to leave from Newquay late afternoon.

'I can't believe I'm going to go on a private plane,' said Cat. 'I haven't even ever been on a normal plane. How many of us are there?'

'Eight. Meena – to chaperone us all – and Ollie and his mates, who are all coming down on Thursday night,' I began.

'But won't your mum suspect if she sees them?' Becca interrupted. We were at her house on Saturday morning going through her wardrobe for the thousandth time.

'No. She knows they're off school on Friday so just thinks they're down for a long weekend.'

'Wasn't one of them down last year for your mum's Christmas party?' Squidge asked.

'Yes. Er . . . Michael was.'

Squidge looked out into the distance for a few moments and looked thoughtful. 'Yeah. I remember him. Good-looking guy. He's . . . well, he's the kind I thought you'd always go for.'

I punched him. 'Don't be mad . . .'

'Are his parents loaded too?' he asked.

'I think they do OK. I think his dad has his own production company.'

'TV?' asked Squidge.

I nodded. It made me feel uncomfortable talking about Michael, and I wanted to get off the subject before I blushed or did something stupid to give myself away.

'TV company, huh? More interesting than what my dad does. Being a mechanic isn't exactly mind-blowing stuff.'

'Yes it is,' I said. 'Your dad's the most important man in the village. Cat told me that when I first moved down here. And your mum's the most important woman. Transport and good hair. We'd be lost without them.'

'Not very glamorous, though,' said Squidge with a wistful look.

'She's incredibly glamorous, your mum,' said Cat. 'A blonde babe.'

'Nah,' said Squidge. 'Ordinary. My folks are ordinary.'

I'd never heard Squidge talk like this before, as if he was embarrassed by his background. It was strange, as I'd always thought that I was the one with the hang-up about being ordinary.

'Go over the whole itinerary again,' said Becca, getting out her notebook. 'I want to write it all down so I don't forget.'

I laughed. 'We'll all be together. You're not going to forget or get forgotten and anyway, haven't you got the print-out that Susie did for us all. That has everything on it.'

'I know. Just go over it again. I like hearing.'

'OK. Next Friday afternoon, straight after school, you all come back with me to Barton Hall where we will be picked up and driven to the airport in Newquay, from where we fly to Marrakech. The flight is just over three hours and we have time on our side as they're an hour behind us over there.'

'So we need to have everything ready and packed on Thursday,' said Squidge. 'I must check that all my camera batteries are charged and that I have a spare memory card – I don't want to run out when we get there.'

'Does your mum know anything yet, Lia?' asked Cat.

'She suspected something was up because of all the phone calls coming in so Dad told her half the truth. He told her that he's booked them a weekend away in Morocco at the hotel where they met. She was really pleased and I think she believes that that is it. That's the secret. I don't think she has a clue that we're all going too.'

'Are they going by private plane?' asked Cat.

I shook my head. 'Dad's going to take Mum up to London early on Friday to get her out of the way. Then they're flying first class with a commercial airline from Gatwick. He's going to whisk her out to tea as soon as they get there. We check into Riad Rhoul as soon as we arrive and hide until Dad tells us. He knows the times that the rest of the guests will be arriving. He's going to tell Mum that he's taking her for dinner somewhere special and will suggest a drink at the roof terrace bar in the hotel before they go – and that's where we'll all be.'

'Top,' said Squidge. 'Couldn't have organised it better myself!'

'Saturday will be sight-seeing,' I said. 'Susie's printed out some interesting places for us to choose from. We can go to the souk, we can hang out by the pool, we can visit some of the old palaces . . .'

'Let's do everything,' said Squidge. 'I want to see as much as I can. I'm going to get up at five o'clock on Saturday morning and go out and photograph before all the tourists arrive.'

'On the Saturday evening, Dad's booked everyone in for a tourist event called Fantasia. It sounds like fun.'

Cat picked up Susie's information sheet and read. '*An evening of Moroccan cuisine and entertainment, finishing with an extravagant show of Arabian horses.* Now, that's something you don't get to see down Whitsand Beach. It's going to be sooooo cool.'

'I know. It just gets better and better,' said Squidge. 'Horses. And I bet there will be firelight. Wow. Can you imagine the shots I'm going to be able to get?'

'Then on Sunday once again, guests can choose either between a trip into the Atlas mountains for lunch or a trip to a little fishing port for lunch in a hotel there. Both places are a couple of hours' drive away so it's a chance to see something of the countryside and then, early evening, we fly back.'

'Essoo . . .?' asked Cat as she looked over the agenda. 'How do you say the name of the fishing port place?'

'Essaouira,' I said. 'Es–ah–oo–weara. Or something like that.'

I'd looked it up on the Internet as soon as I'd heard that we had a chance to go there and it looked heavenly. Long white beaches by a working fishing port, a walled town, little alleyways full of stalls selling all sorts. I wanted to go there rather than up into the mountains as it would be perfect after the hustle and bustle of Marrakech. I could just imagine Squidge and me, hand in hand strolling along the beach in the sun. I hoped that he wouldn't pick to do the mountain trip.

'Essaouira was the place where all the artists and musicians and writers used to hang out in the Sixties and Seventies,' I said. 'Jimi Hendrix, Frank Zappa and Jefferson Airplane – apparently, they all went there. Even my dad was there for a brief time when he was a kid. Gran and Grandad Axford were doing the hippie trail. Dad said he can remember Hendrix being in Essaouira although he didn't stay there long.'

'Your family is just soooo cool,' said Cat. 'My gran and grandad never even left Cornwall.'

Squidge's jaw dropped. 'Hendrix? Zappa? Can't wait, can't wait, can't wait.'

On Sunday, it was Cat's turn for us to go through her wardrobe and pick out what she should take. Becca was so funny because she lay on the floor most of the time we were there, doing abdominal exercises.

'If I'm going to have to wear a bikini in front of all those boys, I want to look halfway decent,' she panted as she did her tummy curls.

'I don't know what you worry about,' I said. 'You have an amazing body.' She does. She's tall and curvy as opposed to me, who is tall and flat-chested. I look like a boy in a bikini.

Cat looked at her watch. 'Five more days, eleven more hours . . .'

'Twenty-five more minutes,' said Becca. 'Time seems to have been going so slow since we found out. I can't wait for Friday to come round.'

We hadn't seen much of Mac. His mother really had meant business when she said that she wanted him to study, and he hadn't been allowed out, not once. In a way, that wasn't a bad thing because I think hearing the rest of us talk non-stop about the trip would only have made him feel left out. Squidge had made sure that he'd been round to see him when he could and they'd studied for their exams together. His parents had a much more laidback approach to homework though and left it up to Squidge to set his own study times. Their method seemed to work as Squidge worked hard in most of his spare time.

On Monday night, he came home with me after school for a quick supper and to talk over last-minute details for the trip.

He sat on the window seat in my room while I pulled out the case that I had hidden under my bed. I'd started packing days ago and kept adding things then taking them out.

Squidge laughed when he saw me swap the sundress I wanted to take for the third time.

'You will look fabulous whatever you wear,' he said. 'You should do a checklist, you know; write it all out so that you know you haven't forgotten anything. Camera, bikini, dress, sunglasses . . .'

'Sunglasses!' I said. 'I must put them in.'

I went to my drawer and rummaged about and pulled out my favourite pair. I'd bought them a few months ago and they were the best glasses I'd ever had. Big and black and they felt really comfortable. However, when I pulled them out from where they'd been shoved in the drawer, I noticed a little crack in the right lens.

'Oh no. They're broken!'

Squidge got up and took them from me. 'Yep. Think they are. Haven't you got any others you can take?'

I shook my head. 'Not as nice. Those are my favourites. I got them from the post office in Kingsand.'

Squidge nodded. 'Yeah, they have some good stuff in there. She's probably got some more the same. Want me to go and look?'

'Would you?'

'Yeah. I could get some tomorrow after school.'

I suppose my face showed my disappointment. 'I don't suppose we could go now. We're leaving on Friday so that doesn't give us much time and I want to be sure that she has them otherwise I'll have to go over to Plymouth tomorrow . . .'

'Nah,' said Squidge. 'I shouldn't worry. There will be shops at the airport. You can get some there if the post office is sold out.'

'But we're not going to have time to hang about. It won't be like flying normally. Private plane. You drive straight up and get on. And anyway, Newquay's a small airport; they might not have shops and, if they do, they might not have nice glasses on sale. Oh, finking stinking nuisance . . .'

Squidge stood up. 'Tell you what. I'll go for you now.'

'No. You don't have to do that . . .'

'No problem,' said Squidge as he picked up the broken glasses. 'I'll take these with me so I'm sure to get the right ones and I'll be back in no time. What time will supper be?'

'In about half an hour.'

'It will take twenty minutes tops on my bike.'

'No really, don't, Squidge. I was just ranting as I'm so cross I broke my favourites. It doesn't matter . . .'

But he was already heading for the door. 'Be back in a tick,' he said. And with that, he was off. A man on a mission.

As I waited for him to come back, I tried on a few more clothes. So many decisions. Whether to take my turquoise bikini or my black swimsuit. Or both. My striped sarong or the Indian one that matches my bikini. Or both.

It was only when Meena called up that it was supper time that I realised that Squidge had been gone over half an hour. I quickly gave his mobile a call to see how long he would be but it was on voice mail. Grrrr, I thought. I really must talk to him about always leaving his phone off. But it must mean that he's on his way back.

I went down to the kitchen and told Meena that Squidge was on his way and I'd like to wait for him.

I went into the red room and looked out of the window and down the drive to see if there was any sign of him but it was empty apart from Max and Molly cavorting around.

I checked my watch. Forty minutes had passed.

I called his house in case he'd dropped in for something while he was down in the village.

'No, love,' said Mrs Squires. 'He said he would be up at yours for his supper. So where is he?'

'Oh probably on his way back. He went into the village to fetch something.'

After my call to his mum, I tried his mobile again.

Still on voice mail. And by now it was getting close to an hour that he'd been gone.

I tried calling Mac but he was none the wiser and like Mrs Squires thought that Squidge was with me.

An hour and a half went by and I was starting to get hungry waiting for Squidge.

I had just gone into the kitchen to get some juice when I heard the phone ring. Mum got to it before I did.

'It will be for me,' I said as I walked towards her but then something in the tone of her voice and her expression made me stop.

'. . . yes, yes. I'll tell her,' said Mum into the receiver.

'What? What's happened?' I asked, as a feeling of dread came over me.

Mum put the phone down and turned to me. 'There's been an accident . . .'

'Oh God. Squidge?'

Mum nodded. 'An ambulance was called and he's been taken to the hospital.'

6 Hospital

I COULD HARDLY BREATHE.

'Is he OK?' I asked.

'They don't know yet,' Mum answered. 'That was his dad on the phone and he said that he'd call as soon as they know anything.'

'Which hospital have they taken him to?'

'Torpoint.'

'I have to go. Will you take me, Mum? Please. *Please*. I can't sit here and wait.'

This can't be happening, I thought. It felt unreal and I felt numb, couldn't take it in. Oh God please let him be OK, I prayed.

Mum put her arms around me. 'Hey, come on. We don't know what happened. He might be fine.'

'He might not be. We don't know. Please, Mum. Let's go.'

Mum nodded. 'Of course. I'll go and get the car,' she said.

On the way to the hospital, my imagination ran riot and images of Squidge broken and bruised played through my mind. What could possibly have happened? And where? I made Mum repeat to me over and over what Squidge's dad had said in case I'd missed something but no, it seemed that Mr Squires knew very little.

'I bet he took a corner too fast and came off his bike,' I said. 'He's always doing that. I bet that's what it is. He's broken something.'

'Probably,' said Mum but she sounded as worried as I felt.

When we got to the hospital, we raced to Accident and Emergency and I quickly scanned the people waiting in the hope that we'd see Squidge sitting there, wearing a big sheepish grin and nothing the matter with him except a sprained wrist.

But there was no sign of him or any of his family.

Mum went up to the reception desk and spoke to a lady sitting behind there.

'Please could you help us? We're looking for a boy,

sixteen years old. He was in an accident and was brought in maybe half an hour ago.'

'Name?'

'Mrs Axford.'

'No. The boy's name.'

'Oh. Course. Sorry. Jack Squires.'

The lady scanned the computer to her right and then jerked her chin towards double doors on the left. 'Through there. Straight on then left at the bottom. The doctors are with him now and his family are in the waiting area there. You can join them if you like.'

Doctors with him? I thought as I reminded myself to keep breathing. Oh God, oh God. Oh please, please let him be OK.

The corridor which led to where we'd been sent was lined with chairs filled with worried-looking people, probably patients' relatives. They looked so pale in the bright fluorescent light. I hate hospitals, I thought. I hate the suffocating disinfectant-mixed-with-boiled-vegetables smell. I hate the unnatural light. I hate the atmosphere of anxiety. I hate to think that Squidge is in here and is hurt.

As we turned the corner, we knew we'd found the right area – at the far end of the corridor, we could see Mrs and Mr Squires and Will, Squidge's younger brother. The sight of them sitting there in silence made my eyes well up with tears. It was unlike them to be so quiet as usually whenever the Squires family was around, it meant noise, laughter and everyone talking at once.

Mr Squires nodded as soon as he saw us approaching. He looked worn out, like he'd aged about ten years.

'How is he?' I asked when we reached them.

Mr Squires shrugged his shoulders and opened his palms as if to say we don't know.

'No one will tell us anything,' said Will in a solemn voice. 'Bloody doctors don't realise they're dealing with human beings, not lumps of meat.'

His dad put his arm round him. 'Hey now, don't swear, lad.'

'But you did,' said Will.

Mr Squires looked at his wife and rolled his eyes and she half smiled back at him. I got the feeling that Will had just repeated something that he'd heard his father say earlier.

'Do you know what happened yet?' Mum asked.

'The ambulance men said that there was an accident,' Mrs Squires replied. 'At the crossroads at the top of Kingsand village. They say a car was coming down the hill and went straight . . .' Her voice began to wobble and Mr Squires put his arm round her.

'We're not sure what happened,' he continued for her. 'Seems there was a crash between a car and Squidge on his bike. We don't know how bad it is yet as no one will give us the details. He's in with a couple of doctors at the moment.'

I felt like I was going to faint as my ears began to buzz and I was still finding it hard to breathe. This is all my fault, I kept thinking, all my fault.

'What was Squidge doing down in the village?' asked Mr Squires, as if he'd picked up on my thoughts.

'Oh . . .' I didn't know what to say. Mum was standing there and if I said that Squidge had gone to get me sunglasses for the Morocco trip, Dad's surprise would be ruined. But did that even matter anymore? If Squidge was badly hurt, there might not even be a Morocco trip. And if Squidge's parents knew he'd gone to fetch something for me then they might blame me for the accident and hate me forever. And they'd be right to as it was my fault. 'I . . . er . . .'

'She doesn't know, love,' said Mrs Squires to her husband. 'She called me . . . oh must have been half an hour before the accident, remember, Lia? You rang to ask if I knew where Squidge was and I said I thought he was with you and . . .'

Luckily my inquisition was interrupted and I didn't have

to think about what to say as a young doctor came out of a nearby room and walked towards us.

'Mr and Mrs Squires?'

Squidge's mum and dad nodded, stood up. Mr Squires took his wife's hand and squeezed it. 'Yes. That's us. Is he going to be all right?'

The doctor shifted about on his feet and looked down at them. 'We can't say for certain yet. He's concussed so we're running tests to see if there's any lasting damage. I'm so sorry I can't tell you more at present. We should know within the hour. Apart from that, he's broken his left leg, his collarbone is fractured and his wrist is sprained and . . . well, we're still doing tests to make sure that his spine hasn't been damaged as it appears that he took a knock to his back when he came off the bike.'

Mrs Squires let out a moan and reached for her husband.

I felt the corridor start to spin and sat down on the nearest chair. Mum immediately sat next to me and put her arm round me.

'I'm so sorry,' said the doctor. 'We'll let you know as soon as we can.'

'Can I see him?' asked Mrs Squires.

The doctor hesitated and quickly glanced at all of us, then he nodded. 'Five minutes as we still have tests to do.'

Mrs Squires quickly disappeared into the room that the doctor had just come out of. The rest of us sat outside in silence waiting until I couldn't bear it any longer.

'I'm going to phone Cat, Becca and Mac,' I said to the others.

'Good idea,' said Mr Squires. 'We ought to let them know. Yes. Good. In fact, I ought to make a few calls too, let people know.'

'You can't use your mobile in here,' Will piped up. 'It can interfere with the machines and blow them up and make people explode.' He pointed to a poster saying that mobiles weren't allowed.

'I know that,' I said. 'I'm going outside.'

Once outside, I called Mac, Cat and Becca and each of them was horrified when they heard the news. I tried to reassure them that there was nothing that they could do but, like me, each of them wanted to be where Squidge was.

When I got back inside, I saw that Mum was holding Mrs Squires's hand.

'What's happened?' I asked. 'Has something else happened? Where's Squidge's dad?'

Will pointed at the room. 'He's having a visit with Squidge. Doctor said we could have a few minutes each.'

'How was he?' I asked Mrs Squires.

She shook her head. Her eyes were red from crying. 'He . . . he looks so peaceful. Like he's sleeping. His leg's all trundled up and his arm's in a cast. There are all these machines . . . Oh God, please let him wake up.'

A moment later, Mr Squires came out and sat heavily beside his wife.

'Can I go in?' I asked and Mr Squires nodded but, just as I was about to open the door to Squidge's room, a doctor came up behind me, put his hand on my shoulder and pulled me back. 'Maybe later,' he said. 'We have to finish our tests.'

I nodded and went back to join the others.

After a while Mr Squires stood up. 'I can't stand this. I'm going to phone around . . .'

Mum also stood up. 'And I'll go and get some coffees. Who wants something?'

Everyone shook their head. No one wanted anything.

'Ah well,' said Mum. 'You might change your minds later.'

As the evening went on, the hospital corridor began to fill up with friends and relatives. Cat. Becca. Mac. Cat's dad. Squidge's aunts. Uncles. More aunts and uncles. Squidge calls his family 'the tribe' as there are so many of them. Sometimes it seemed like they ran the whole of the Rame peninsula. One ran the pub, another the dry cleaners, another the bakery and so on. Squidge would be glad to know that they were all here. Oh please please, God, let him come round. And please God let him be all right.

Cups of coffee were bought, drunk. Tears were shed. Anxieties shared. Everything seemed unreal, like time had stopped still and we were all in some strange dream. Or nightmare.

'Squidge is really popular, isn't he?' said Mac as Squidge's Uncle Ed pitched up.

I nodded. I didn't feel like talking much.

After about half an hour, the door to Squidge's room opened again and the doctor came out. He looked tired and surprised as so many pairs of eyes turned to look at him questioningly.

'I think he's going to make a full recovery,' he said and there was a collective sigh. 'A few broken bones, a few nasty bruises and he's still concussed but we're confident that there's no lasting damage.'

'What about his spine?' asked Mr Squires. 'Will he be able to walk?'

The doctor nodded. 'When the broken bone in his leg heals, yes, he will be able to walk.'

'Oh thank God,' said Mrs Squires.

'Can I see him now?' I asked then turned to Mr and Mrs Squires. 'If that's all right with you?'

'Family member?' the doctor asked, directing the question to Squidge's dad.

'Girlfriend,' his dad said, grinning.

'Ah, go on, then. I don't see why not,' said the doctor. 'But don't stay too long.'

He opened the door for me and I crept into a darkened room. It took a moment for my eyes to adjust after the bright light of the corridor but they soon did and there was my Squidge lying there, his leg and arm in casts and wired up to monitors behind the bed. As his mum had said, he looked so peaceful. Like he was asleep. I tiptoed over to the bed and looked for his hand. I gently put my right hand on top of his left.

'I'm so sorry, Squidge. It's all my fault.' I sat on the edge of the bed and brushed his forehead with the tips of my fingers on my left hand. 'Oh please come back to us. Please come back. It's me. Lia. You've been in an accident but you're going to be all right. But please wake up. I'm so sorry.'

But it seemed that Squidge was in the deepest of deep sleeps.

After another minute, the doctor put his head around the door. 'Best leave him for now.'

I got up to leave and leaned across to kiss Squidge lightly on the top of his head. As I moved across, I saw his eyes flicker and he let out a soft groan.

I quickly went to the door, opened it and looked for the doctor who was standing nearby talking to Mr Squires.

'Doctor, doctor,' I called. 'I think he may be coming round.'

There was a louder groan from behind me and as I turned, I saw Squidge move slightly in the bed. And then a louder groan. And then he opened his eyes, looked at the ceiling then tried to turn his head.

'Errrgh . . .' he moaned. 'Galloping gonads. Where the bejesus am I?'

I ran over to the bed. Oh thank you thank you, God.

Squidge was back.

No Go's a No Go

'EVERYTHING WENT INTO SLOW MOTION,' said Squidge as
Mac sat by his side and drew a cartoon down one side of his
leg cast. 'The moment I got hit keeps replaying and
replaying in my head as though a CD has got stuck in
there.'

'It's probably your brain trying to make sense of it,' said
Cat. 'Trying to take it in.'

It was Tuesday night and Cat, Becca, Mac and I had gone
straight to the hospital after school bearing gifts of grapes
(which Becca ate), chocolate (which Cat ate) and a bakewell
tart (most of which Mac ate). Squidge didn't seem to have
much of an appetite but at last he was able to tell us what had
happened, as when he came round last night, the doctors told
everyone to go home and rest so we didn't get to find out.

Squidge was sitting up in bed when we arrived and he looked tons better than he had the previous night. The colour had come back into his cheeks and his eyes looked bright.

'So whose fault was it?' asked Becca.

'Not mine,' said Squidge. 'I don't think the guy was even looking at the road. I think he was looking down into the bay and taking in the view. There were no other cars on the road so I reckon that he thought he could relax. He certainly wasn't looking out for a bike.'

'God! Was he hurt as well?' asked Becca.

Squidge shook his head. 'Just freaked out that he'd hit me, I think. He looked totally shocked when he stopped and realised what had happened. Not as shocked as I was, though!'

I squeezed his hand. 'Well, I'm so glad you're OK . . .'

Squidge grimaced and looked at his leg. 'Call this OK? Broken bones and man I ache every time I move . . .'

'I'm so sorry . . .'

'Lia, for the millionest, squillioneth time, it is *not* your fault. I do not blame you in any way. I blame the plonker who was driving the car for not looking where he was going.'

'Yes, but if I hadn't sent you for the sunglasses . . .'

'You didn't send me. I volunteered, as far as I remember,' he said then looked pleadingly at the others. 'Will you tell her?'

'OK. OK,' I said. 'But I am sorry. So there.'

Squidge shrugged. 'I guess it could have been worse. Thing that really pisses me off is that I can't go to Morocco now. Doctors are keeping me in as they want to do some more tests on my brain or something. OK, so it's a bummer to have a broken leg, etc, etc, but that will mend. But the Morocco trip – that was the chance of a lifetime.'

'I'm not going either now,' I said. 'Not if you're not.'

Four faces registered shock.

'You're not?' asked Squidge. 'Why not?'

'Since when?' said Becca.

'Since Squidge got hurt,' I replied.

'But . . . but . . .' Becca blustered. 'You never said anything at school.'

'I wanted to tell Squidge first.'

Cat and Becca looked disappointed.

'Because I'm not going doesn't mean that you can't go,' I said. 'Your places are still booked. Mum and Dad will understand.'

'No way,' said Cat. 'We can't go without you.'

'Did your mum suss anything yesterday?' asked Squidge.

'I'd hate to think I ruined her surprise.'

I shook my head. 'I was about to tell her everything when I thought that you might not come round but then . . .'

Squidge grinned. 'Ah. Had you all worried some, did I?'

'I'll say,' said Mac. 'Seriously.'

'But you said your mum and dad *will* understand. Does that mean you haven't told them yet?' asked Becca.

I shook my head again. 'Not yet. Well, it's Dad I have to tell, really, and I didn't see him this morning before I left for school. He'd gone out riding.'

'You're mad,' said Squidge. 'You can't not go because of me. Forget it.'

'I can not go and I'm not going. I'll stay here and look after you. And we won't miss out totally. There's still the midsummer party to look forward to.'

Squidge shook his head. 'No. No way. Your no go is a no go. What do you think, Mac?'

Mac shrugged. 'Not up to me, man. Your call.'

'Yeah and I'm not letting this happen,' said Squidge then looked at Cat, Becca, then Mac. 'Can you give us five?'

'Sure,' said Mac and he and the others got up to leave.

'Want a drink or something from the machine?' asked Becca.

'No thanks. Just give us five minutes.'

When they had gone and closed the door, Squidge took my hand and looked into my eyes. 'Remember what we said about always telling the truth? No matter what?'

I nodded.

'Well, this is the truth, Lia. I really don't want you to stay here. What are you going to do? Sit by my bedside and read to me? No way when you could be in Marrakech and Essieooo . . .'

'Essaouira.'

'Yeah. There.'

'But it won't be the same without you. No. I don't want to go now.'

'You have to.'

'Don't.'

'Do.'

'You can't make me.'

'Can.'

'Can't.'

'Can.'

'How?'

Squidge sighed. 'You don't get it, do you? I can't be responsible for you not going and it's not fair that you are laying that on me when I'm in this state.' He lay back on his pillows and groaned a long, loud, theatrical groan. 'Oooooooooh. Argghhhhhhh. Eeeeeeeee. See, physical pain is one thing, but to carry the mental pain of knowing that I have wrecked not only your weekend but your mum's fortieth birthday would be too much. The guilt. The guilt . . .'

'Let me tell you something,' I said. 'Stick with your photography, because I can tell you one thing for sure: you haven't got a future as an actor.'

Sadly my resistance to his amateur dramatics only spurred him on. He put the back of his good hand on his forehead and continued to act as tragically as he possibly could. 'You are very cruel to do this to me. Ooooooohhhh, the m-e-e-e-e-ent-a-a-a-al tort-u-u-u-u-ure. The burden I have to bear. The weight of the world.' (Sigh, heavier sigh.) 'Imagine the damage you would do by playing the martyr and staying behind to tend to my needs, my humble needs. It would make me feel like a failure,' (he looked sadly at his broken leg) 'as well as a cripple. Emasculated. I will probably have to go into counselling for years and years to get over it.'

I had a feeling that I was being manipulated or blackmailed or something, and I also got the feeling that he wasn't going to take no for an answer.

'OK. OK. You win. Anything to stop this dreadful performance. I'll go. I'll go. I wouldn't want to put you in therapy for the rest of your life.'

Squidge sat up again and grinned. 'Good. Because I want you to do something for me.'

'What's that?'

'Take photos for me. Everything. Seeing as I can't go, I'll give you my digital camera to take and you can bring it all back to me.'

'Of course I will. And I'll come and see you every night before I go and I'll be round the minute I get back.'

'Good. And one more thing. The truth thing again. Seriously. I want you to tell me about all of it. What you see, hear, feel, taste and don't hold back because you think I might feel I missed out. I know I'm missing out and that's why I want to hear it all from you when you get back.'

He linked the little finger from his good hand with the little finger from my left and pulled.

'Truth,' he said.

'Truth,' I repeated after him.

'Excellent. Now. Is there any of that bakewell tart left or did Mac scoff the lot?'

8 Morocco Bound

'WAHEY. THIS IS SOOOOOO FANTASTIC,' said Becca, as she draped herself Cleopatra-style across the corner sofa on the plane.

Cat sniffed the air. 'Yeah. And it *smells* so expensive. Like good cologne and leather. And wow, look at that movie screen. It's like a private cinema in here.'

We'd just boarded the plane at Newquay airport and the girls were well impressed. Walnut-panelled walls. Tasteful abstract prints. Honey-coloured leather sofas and chairs arranged around small tables – it was more like being in the lounge of a posh hotel than on an aeroplane.

'Yeah,' I said. 'And there's a DVD library . . .'

'Library!' exclaimed Becca. 'I thought we got a choice of three movies.'

'Not when you go private. That's part of the fun.'

'Yeah,' said Cat picking up a card from the coffee table in front of us. 'And have you seen this menu? Ohmigod. Basically, we can have anything we like. Champagne . . . Dom Pérignon, Cristal . . . Blimey! I wonder if I could get a plain Coke?'

I had to smile at them. They were really enjoying themselves and we hadn't even taken off yet. I'd flown privately loads of times but it was different being with my friends. It was like seeing it all through new eyes.

'I've only flown a few times,' said Becca as she looked around in awe. 'And I can tell you, Cat, it was *nothing* like this. Usually there are about fifty seats, maybe even more all lined up in rows in a space about this size. And you hardly get any leg room so it's bad luck if you're tall. Once I had this enormous guy sitting next to me and he took up his seat and spilled over into mine. I thought I was going to suffocate. But this . . .' She stretched out and curled up her toes. 'This is the business. Luxury. This is how I want to travel from now on.'

'Me too,' said Cat then looked around. 'Where's Meena gone?'

'Probably gone to round the boys up,' I said as I glanced behind me to the door. It was getting close to take-off time and the boys still weren't on board as Jamie wanted to buy shaving stuff at the last minute and they'd dashed off into the airport to see if there was a chemist's in there.

I got up to look around the rest of the plane and found Meena fussing about in the kitchen area, much to the bemusement of the pretty blonde flight attendant in there. 'You don't have to do that, Meena,' I said. 'Come and sit down. This is meant to be a break for you too.'

'Just checking, just checking,' she said as I ushered her back along to the lounge area. 'But it's OK. All in order.'

Meena is a total sweetheart. She must be well into her fifties and has been with us since as far back as I can remember. She looked after all of us as babies, Star, Ollie and me. She's part of our family now, more like an auntie to me than a housekeeper.

When we got back to the lounge area, I saw that the boys had boarded. Ollie was sitting next to Cat and I got Squidge's camera out of my travel bag to take a shot of them as they made such an attractive couple, Ollie with his square handsome face and Cat with her pretty heart-shaped face. Becca was sitting between Jamie and Henry and looking very pleased with herself. I wondered if she fancied either of them. Henry was the better looking of the two: stocky and fair-haired, like Ollie, he is a bit of a heart-throb back in

London where he is the school's star rugby player, but it was Jamie who I thought was most fun to be with. He was smaller than the others with longish brown hair that curled around his collar, and green eyes that took in everything.

Michael was sitting to my right, looking through the DVDs. He glanced up and smiled when he saw me. Michael Bradley. His name still had a strange effect on me, but probably only because I'd written it a thousand times in my notebooks in junior school and later in Years Seven and Eight of secondary. Michael Bradley and Lia Axford. MB and LA. MB loves LA. It seems silly now that I have grown up and moved on. I used to doodle his face in the margins of all my notebooks. Normally, I'm not too good at art but I'd got his features perfect, I'd drawn them so many times. Strong jaw. Dimple in the middle. Wide mouth, slightly plumper lower lip. Straight nose. Velvety brown eyes, silky dark hair with one bit above his right eye that likes to stick up on its own. It had been weird seeing him the night before when the boys arrived down from their school. I wasn't sure what I'd feel. I'd been with Squidge since the last time I'd seen him and hadn't thought about any other boy, never mind Michael. He seemed genuinely pleased to see me again and made a point of letting me know that he was now single and that he and Usha had split up. I made it clear straight from the start that I had a boyfriend.

'Yeah, I heard,' he'd said, leaning towards me, so that I caught his scent. It was Armani, same as Ollie's. 'A boyfriend with his leg in a cast, so I believe he won't be joining us.'

I didn't know what to make of it and if he was teasing or flirting with me. Whichever it was, I was going to remain true to Squidge. My crush on Michael was from when I was a kid, I reminded myself. I've grown up and moved on.

Watching everyone settle in for the flight, I felt a painful tug in my stomach as I couldn't help thinking that Squidge should be here, hand in mine as we took off, enjoying himself too. He'd have loved travelling by private jet.

I began to shoot the interior of the plane.

'Why are you taking pics of the inside of the plane?' asked Ollie as he tried to poke his head into the frame. 'Bit boring, isn't it?'

'For Squidge,' I said. 'I promised him I would photograph all of it right from the start.'

Ollie winked at his mates and, quick as a whistle, he, Jamie and Henry got up, turned away from us, dropped their trousers over their bum cheeks and mooned for the camera.

'There you go then,' said Ollie. 'This will make it more interesting. One of the most beautiful sights imaginable.'

'Oll*ie*,' I cried. '*Grrrrossss.*'

Cat and Becca cracked up laughing while Michael rolled his eyes to the heavens and said, 'Grow up, guys.'

Meena, however, was straight up on her feet.

'Cover up, cover up. Bad boys, bad boys,' she said and smacked the three of them on their backsides like they were toddlers who had misbehaved. This only made the others laugh even more. I made sure I got it all on camera. It would make Squidge laugh too. It was the sort of stupid thing that he and Mac might have done if they were here.

The boys zipped up and sat back down under Meena's disapproving eye and, not long after, the pilot came on board. He introduced himself and his crew, told us a bit about the flight route and time and then disappeared up front.

Soon after, as we took off, I looked out of the window. As we rose upwards, the ground beneath quickly began to recede. Houses and buildings growing smaller and smaller until they looked like tiny rows of boxes and the cars on roads appeared like ants. I turned to look at the lush, green fields disappearing below and behind us and thought that not far away was my poor Squidge all trussed up in his hospital bed in one of the building boxes while we flew higher and higher and further away.

The plane reached cloud level, broke through and I could no longer see the ground. Only a marshmallow landscape of white fluffy clouds and the blue blue sky beyond.

We were on our way.

As we flew, the others chatted and played games. Ollie and Cat settled down to watch a DVD and Becca already seemed to have Jamie and Henry hanging on her every word. She's so good at flirting, I thought as I watched her flick her hair back and bat her eyelashes as she replied to something that Henry said. I wish I could be as cool and confident as she is.

Every now and again, I glanced over at Michael and every time he was watching me. I'd quickly look away then a few minutes later glance back and he was *still* staring. With a quiet smile on his face. It was very unnerving. I wanted to tell him to stop looking at me, but that would only draw the others' attention to us and that was the last thing I wanted. Ollie teasing me for the whole weekend? No thank you.

After a while we started chatting about our lives and school and people we knew. He was easy to talk to. A nice guy. Interesting. Grown up, in a way. Not that Mac or Squidge aren't, just that Michael comes across as older somehow. He told me he wanted to be a journalist and I told him that I was confused and didn't know what I wanted to be. We talked about art, music, movies and at one point, I thought, ooh, this is getting to be a little too comfortable, especially as whenever there is a pause in the conversation, he still looks at me with an intent expression.

I made the excuse of wanting to take some photos out of the window and moved over to another window seat which was away from Michael's gaze where I spent the rest of the flight looking out and daydreaming. It's one of my favourite things to do on planes and on trains. I love the sense of feeling suspended from the world and from my life for a short time. The feeling that I've left one place but haven't reached the next and watching the passing sky, the swirl of clouds or terrain below. Over fields, roads, rivers, mountains and lives so different from mine. I've been so lucky so far and I've been to some amazing places and had some fantastic holidays: Kenya, Cape Town, Botswana, South America, Florida, San Francisco, New York, Thailand, Australia, Europe, we've been pretty well all over the world. We'd even been to North Africa before, to Tunisia. I liked Africa. Some places you can go and it doesn't feel like you're anywhere much different to England. But in Africa, you know that you are. From the moment you see the vast expanse of uninhabited parched brown earth down below from the plane window and then, when you land, feel the warmth of the sun on your skin and breathe the air that smells of spices, herbs, flowers and wood.

The journey took just over three hours and it didn't feel like long before the pilot informed us that we were flying over Casablanca and it was twenty minutes to landing. Fields below became a patchwork of ice cream colours: honey, strawberry, mint, caramel, vanilla and dark cocoa then a city of pink ochre appeared and the plane started to descend. I glanced over at Cat who was leaning on Ollie's shoulder and he was holding her hand. I wondered if she'd felt nervous with this being her first time flying. If she had been, she certainly hadn't shown it but I knew Cat. I knew she could hold her true feelings in and if she'd been scared at all, she wouldn't have wanted the boys to know.

Becca was playing a card game with Jamie and Henry and she seemed to be winning.

Meena was dozing in her chair.

And Michael was still watching me. I immediately turned away and glanced at the floor then thought, hey, I'm not the kid that used to be in awe and intimidated by him. I'm fourteen now. I lifted my head, turned round and looked right back at him as though challenging him to look away. Our eyes held contact and a bolt of electricity shot through me. He felt it too. I knew he did because his quiet smile spread into a grin and he raised an eyebrow as if to acknowledge what had happened.

I broke his gaze and found Squidge's camera once more.

'I'm going to film what the land looks like from up here for Squidge,' I said to Michael. 'It's so different from the green of England, don't you think?'

Michael nodded. 'Ah yes Lia,' he said. 'Yes.'

I turned away and began to shoot out of the window. I felt confused and cross but I didn't know whether it was with Michael or myself. How could I feel something that strong when I had a boyfriend? A boyfriend I *really* liked and wouldn't hurt for anything. I remembered what he'd made me promise about always telling the truth. If that was to be the case then I would have to do my best to keep away from Michael Bradley once we got off the plane. It was Squidge and Lia now. Not Michael and Lia.

9 *Marrakech*

ANY THOUGHTS OF MICHAEL or even Squidge disappeared as soon as we landed and everything went into superspeed – the blast of heat as we got off the plane, the limo picking us up, Jamie and Henry doing the obligatory standing up through the sun roof to wave at people as we passed by, mopeds, bikes, taxis, vans – the mad hot hustle bustle of traffic on the roads into Marrakech, arriving at the hotel, meeting up with Star, Rhiannon and George who had got there on the earlier flight from London. Saying hi to the other guests (also on the flight from London), a quick tour of the hotel, Cat's eyes shining bright as she took it all in, Becca happy happy to be there, getting showered, changed and quickly into place at the roof terrace bar ready to surprise Mum. Phew. But we made it.

It looked heavenly up there. The sky was soft with the fading light, pastel pink, blue and silver. At the back of the terrace, a low cedarwood table had been laid with crystal, cutlery and candles inside a large Arabian tent. Around the table were plush purple and gold-threaded cushions and on the floor were scattered rugs in the Moroccan colours of red, burgundy and gold. It looked like a table set for a sheikh and his harem. Around the rest of the terrace, soft muslin curtains in reds and purples floated in the evening breeze and at the front above a bar area, a purple silk canopy wafted into the sky. It felt so romantic and I knew Mum was going to love it.

Becca looked at her watch, then out over the ochre roofs of houses in the medina (the market area) that stretched into the distance. 'It's amazing, isn't it? Like a dream.'

'Did you put your watch back?' asked Cat.

Becca nodded. 'Nine p.m. UK time. Eight p.m. here and look at where we are! I have to keep pinching myself!'

'And everyone is so stunning,' said Cat as she watched the guests arrive up the stairs on to the terrace.

Everyone had dressed up for the occasion and was looking their Oscar best. Poor Squidge, I thought, he's probably bored out of his mind right now cooped up in bed watching the soaps on telly and having some horrible hospital dinner instead of being here in this exotic tent in the sky ready to eat a feast fit for a king. I quickly took shots of the room with the camera so that he'd be able to see it all when I got back but I doubted that he'd be able to get the atmosphere. Everyone was in such a good mood and the air was buzzing with anticipation.

Cat and Becca looked fabulous. Becca had been to a beauty salon in the week and had one of those spray tan treatments that make you seem as though you've been on holiday for a week. She was wearing a turquoise halter top that made her eyes look the same colour, black trousers, and she'd swept her hair up so that she looked really grown up and sophisticated. Cat was wearing an amazing pink and red tie-dye corset top, a black skirt and a pair of Emma Hope red heels that my sister Star had given her last Christmas. She looked so pretty and so happy and Ollie couldn't take his eyes off her (and neither could Jamie – I got him on camera with his jaw hanging open). And I was wearing my short silver silk dress. I wore it because it's Squidge's favourite and he asked me to wear it so that he could imagine me in it. Personally I thought it accentuated my lack of chest but Cat and Becca said it looked great.

Across the terrace, Star suddenly stood up from her bar

stool, put her mobile phone into her bag then lightly struck a glass with a fork so that it made a 'ting' sound. The terrace grew quiet.

'Dad's just called,' she said. 'They've arrived back in the hotel and he's bringing her up here in a few minutes. Now don't forget, she thinks that they're having a quiet romantic supper up here, just the two of them, so everybody hide and when I cough, jump out.'

Everyone dived behind the curtains that lined the terrace while I took as many photos as I could of them all disappearing.

'Come on, Lia,' called Star. 'They'll be here in a sec.'

Most places were taken so I quickly stepped towards the bar area and behind a curtain that led to a tiny balcony overlooking the gardens in the courtyard below. Michael had got there before me and was wedged up against the wall. 'Not much room in here,' he said and pulled me close to him. 'Squeeze in.'

I pulled away. 'Oh! It's OK. I'll find somewhere else.'

'No time,' he said. 'Come on. Squeeze close and I'll put my arms around your waist.'

I knew that he was right and this wasn't the time to be precious or prissy so I leaned back against him so that I couldn't be seen from the terrace. We were so close I could feel his breath on my skin. I felt myself turn to liquid. It felt so perfect, the stunning sky, the scented breeze, my fantasy boy . . .

'You smell gorgeous,' he said as he lifted my hair and nuzzled behind my ear and inhaled the Calvin Klein perfume I'd dabbed on earlier.

Behind my ear is one of my most ticklish spots and I jumped and accidentally elbowed Michael in the stomach.

'Owww,' he groaned.

'Sorry. Ticklish neck,' I whispered.

'Sorry,' he said and nuzzled a bit more.

And then I got the giggles.

'Shhh,' whispered Michael.

'Shhh yourself,' I whispered back.

'You started it.'

'Did not. You did. Nuzzling my neck. But it tickles. Can't help it.'

'Oh really?' he said and started nuzzling again plus nibbling my ear a little.

It felt divine and my knees began to buckle. 'Stop it . . .'

Michael pulled back. 'Sorry. OK. Quiet now.'

The only sound was the distant sound of traffic and Michael's steady breathing and then, from somewhere behind one of the curtains close to us, we heard a soft *thwpp*.

Michael laughed. 'Someone's let one go. Glad they're not in here with us . . .'

'Oops,' we heard a male voice say. I think it was Jamie but whoever it was, it started us off giggling again and soon the pair of us were in agony trying to hold it in. Michael had tears running down his cheeks, he was trying so hard. Luckily we didn't have to wait for too long because we heard footsteps then Dad's voice.

'Here we are. What do you think?' he asked.

'Oh, Zac,' we heard Mum say. 'It's simply beautiful up here . . . but . . . are you sure we're in the right place? That table looks as though it's set for a party.'

And then Star gave the signal cough and we all jumped out.

'Ta-daaaaaah,' I cried.

'Surprise!' called the others. 'Happy birthday.'

Mum looked totally astonished as she took in all the faces she knew standing there in front of her. 'Jamie . . . Lia . . . Star . . . Ollie . . . George . . . Rhiannon. But . . . How did you all get here? And Lia . . . I saw you off to school this morning . . . How . . .?'

Dad laughed. 'Happy birthday, darling.'

'Yes, happy birthday, Mum,' said Ollie.

'I hope you don't mind,' said Dad. 'I know you said that you didn't want a big party.'

'But how did they all get here?' asked Mum.

'Magic carpet,' said Dad. 'Sure you don't mind?'

He needn't have asked. You could tell by Mum's face that she was delighted. 'This is perfect. Just perfect. I just didn't want a big party that *I'd* end up organising but no, this is perfect.'

Waiters appeared from the bar area and up the stairs. Champagne bottles started popping, trays of wonderful canapés started circulating and the sound of laughter rang out across the rooftops.

It was only when Michael came to stand by me and put his arm round my waist that I realised that in all the excitement I'd forgotten to get Mum's reaction on camera.

How was I going to explain to Squidge that I'd missed the most important moment of the whole trip?

Fantasia

10

'ER, OLLIE . . .'

'Yeah?' he called back from the bathroom where I could hear that he was taking a shower.

'What are you boys doing this morning?' I asked.

'Jamie wants to see the Majorelle Gardens. Apparently they're fabulous. Mum and Dad are coming too. And then maybe one of the palaces. What are you girls doing?'

'Not sure yet,' I called back as I stepped into the corridor and scurried back to our room before he could question me any further. Whatever happens, I thought, I need to be as far away from Michael Bradley as possible. I'd let my guard down last night and I couldn't risk letting it happen again.

'Room service, ma'am,' said a pretty Moroccan girl

wheeling a trolley of food down the corridor and stopping outside my room at the same time as I did.

'Thanks,' I said and opened the door so that she could wheel the trolley inside.

I gave her a few dirhams and took the breakfast tray out through the open french windows and on to the little balcony that was adjacent to the room. The hotel was a lovely place to stay. It was right in the heart of the medina and such a surprise when you got inside. It was located on a busy bustling lane which was lined with shops and stalls but, once you stepped inside the huge gate-style door in the high wall, it was peaceful, cool and quiet, and more like a spacious private house than an hotel. It was decorated in the traditional Moroccan style with colourful mosaic tiles on the floors and walls to keep it cool and painted panels of wood up on the ceilings. The Moroccans call these type of houses *riads*, which means a house that doesn't have a window looking out on the street but looks inwards to a central courtyard with a garden instead. This one had a garden *and* a pool in the middle. Cat and Becca loved it.

We'd opted to share a suite even though Dad said that we could have one each but we all wanted to have a Moroccan sleepover. We'd stayed up until three o'clock in the morning talking about the party and the boys and who fancied who. Becca is definitely leaning towards Henry (judging by the snogathon they had on one of the balconies) and I reckon that even with Ollie here, Cat has taken a bit of a shine to Jamie. I don't know if she realises herself yet. She spent a lot of the evening dancing with Ollie but she sat next to Jamie at dinner and I don't think I've ever seen her laugh as much in anyone's company apart from Squidge's. I hadn't told them what I'd felt while hiding with Michael. I felt that if I told anyone, it would become more real whereas if I kept it to myself, I could pretend that it hadn't happened.

Yesterday had been confusing with Michael. I couldn't deny that there was something there between us and I knew that he felt it too. He was majorly fanciable, there was no denying that. I remember when I was little and he used to come over, I used to feel like a fan when they see their pin-up celebrity. That hadn't changed but it didn't mean that I fancied him more than Squidge or regretted that I couldn't follow things up with Michael. I liked both of them but Squidge was my boyfriend and I wasn't going to cheat on him just because he wasn't here and Michael was.

Cat and Becca had both gone down to breakfast in the dining room but I'd decided to have it in our room because I didn't want to bump into Michael. My plan was to avoid him for as much of the trip as possible. I would hang out with the girls today while the boys did their sightseeing. This evening, I'd stay in the hotel when everyone went to the Fantasia night. And tomorrow, I'd go to Essaouira as I'd heard that the boys were going the opposite way and going up to the foothills of the Atlas mountains. And then it would all be over. I'd fly back to Newquay with Mum, Dad, Meena and the girls. And Michael would fly back with Ollie, Jamie and Henry on the London-bound plane as they had to be back for school there on Monday morning. Sorted. No damage would be done. No need to tell a lie to Squidge.

I lifted the silver covers off my breakfast to find a plate of fruits (melon, apricots, kiwi), a plate of cheese and a basket of croissants. Also on the tray was a cafetière of coffee, a small jug of milk and a glass of freshly squeezed orange juice. Squidge would have loved this. Sitting here in the sun on a private balcony in this lovely hotel looking out at the palm trees and flowered shrubs in the courtyard. It felt wonderful; all I could hear was a cacophony of birdsong from the many tiny birds in the garden and, in the distance, the occasional wailing sound of people being called to the mosque. If I closed my eyes, I could see Squidge sitting opposite me as he should have been, a big smile on his face. That was one of the things I loved about Squidge. He was always smiling. He was such a happy person. Always enthusiastic and endlessly curious. It was infectious and being with him always made me feel good.

I went back into the room and got the camera to take a few shots of the peaceful breakfast scene in the shade on the balcony and then the quiet of the courtyard and gardens below. Squidge was always telling me that good films were about contrast and that it was important to follow an action scene with a slower one. I'd show him that I had been listening with my photo story. The party was my action scene (I started taking pics again after missing Mum's reaction and got most of the dinner, party and disco) and now, the morning after was my quiet scene. And then I'd go out and shoot the busy colourful scenes around the main square of Jemaa-el-Fna. With a bit of luck, he wouldn't ask why I had missed the moment we all jumped out to surprise Mum.

My plan to avoid Michael worked perfectly. I watched Mum, Dad and the boys through the open door from behind a pillar in the reception. They got into a couple of taxis and set off for the gardens, and then it was off with the girls to Jemaa-el-Fna. The sun was beating down and the lanes on the way there were a constant bustling stream of pedestrians, mopeds, bicycles, donkeys, mules and carts.

Quite a shock after the oasis of the *riad* and I made sure I got it all on camera for Squidge.

When we reached the square, the next few hours were taken up with exploring the souks and shopping – and what a great experience it was! Star and Rhiannon came with us and together we explored the maze of stalls. Everything was on sale there: spices, gorgeous Ali Baba lamps in every colour and every size, rugs, bedspreads, cushions, clothes, shoes, bags, belts, jewellery, pottery, silver and glass bottles that shone like jewels, scarves, little wooden boxes to keep trinkets in. Stallholders eager to sell their wares called us over at every turn: 'Fatima, Fatima, over here. Only looking. I give you good price. Genuine Berber. Good quality. Please. Just for looking.' And it smelled so exotic: a mixture of cedarwood, barbecued meat, fresh bread, honey, mint, heat, spices and donkey poo! I wished I could capture the scent on film as it was part of the experience of being there.

By three o'clock, we were laden down with bags of all sorts of purchases.

'Don't forget you'll have to carry that on the plane,' said Star as Rhiannon went to purchase an enormous blue- and yellow-coloured bowl. 'It will break if you put it in your suitcase.'

Rhiannon laughed. 'Ohmigod, yes. I hadn't thought of that!'

Cat bought a wallet for her dad, some soft pale blue leather slippers for his girlfriend Jen, wooden snakes that moved like real ones for her brothers Joe and Luke and a lovely turquoise glass perfume bottle for her little sister Emma. Becca bought her mum some silver and coral earrings and her dad a book on Marrakech. I wanted to get something for Squidge. Something that was really Moroccan and that he could treasure.

'You really like this guy, don't you?' asked Rhiannon as we scoured the stalls for the perfect gift.

I nodded. 'He should be here with us. I keep thinking that it's my fault that he's not. He went to fetch something for me and that's when it happened . . .'

Star put her arm round me. 'You can't keep blaming yourself, Lia. Knowing him the little that I do, I don't think that Squidge would want you to. He'd want you to have the best time you can.'

'I guess,' I said. But I couldn't help feeling guilty knowing that I was walking around having a great time when he was still cooped up in bed and all because of me. No memento would ever be as good as having the experience of this place.

At that moment, we walked past a stall selling CDs and the stallholder beckoned us in to listen. The Moroccan music that was blasting out from his stall gave me an idea. Squidge had asked me to be his eyes. I would be his other senses too. His ears. His nose. I'd buy him a CD of Moroccan music so that I could take him the sounds of the place. And if I bought spices and collected flowers and fresh mint from the garden then put them in one of the many cedarwood boxes on sale everywhere, then he'd get the smell of the place. I thought he'd like that better than a wallet or T-shirt saying, *Morocco*.

For the evening, Dad had booked our group to attend a local tourist event called Fantasia and when we got back to the hotel, most of the guests were in their rooms getting ready. It was to be held in a fantasy village outside Marrakech and a coach had been booked to pick everyone up.

As Cat and Becca got ready, I lay on my bed and tried Squidge's mobile. It was still on voice mail so I presumed that meant that he was still in the hospital. To check, I also dialled his home phone number in the hope of getting an update from his mum and dad but no one picked up. They might be visiting Squidge, I thought as I put my phone away.

As Becca and Cat tried on the outfits they had brought, I reviewed the photos that I had taken on the digital camera in the afternoon. Squidge would be pleased. I'd got a few inside the market and outside the square and I think I'd captured the hustle bustle atmosphere of the stalls taking up every available space. I'd put the camera on its video mode for a short while and kept the sound on so that he could hear the noise of the place and the common cry from just about every stallholder as they beckoned us in to look at their wares: 'Hey, just a look. It costs nothing to look.'

'Why aren't you getting dressed?' asked Becca as she came out of the shower with her wet hair dripping down her back.

'Oh. Not going,' I said.

Cat was sitting at the dressing table drying her hair. She turned off the hairdryer. 'You're not coming?'

'Why not?' asked Becca.

'Oh, just fancy an early night and I love being at the hotel . . .'

'Are you *mad*?' asked Becca. 'I wouldn't miss one single tiny bit of this trip. It's all been so brilliant and it keeps getting better.'

She padded back into the shower room and I went back

to looking at my photos. Cat came and sat on the end of my bed.

'OK. So what's going on?' she asked.

'What do you mean?'

'You can't fool me,' she said. 'It's Michael, isn't it? You told me that you were worried about him being here. Has something happened?'

'No. *No*. Well not exactly. A few vibey things. You know . . .'

Cat nodded. 'So what's the problem?'

'No problem.'

Cat put her hand on my arm. 'You can trust me, Lia. I won't blab my mouth off.'

She was looking at me with such genuine concern that I decided to tell her. 'I swore to Squidge that I'd tell him the truth about everything. Everything that happens on the trip. I want to be able to do that.'

'And you will,' said Cat. 'Listen. What Star said earlier is true. Squidge wouldn't want you missing out on anything on his account. Really. How would you explain why you missed the Fantasia? Come on, Lia, you have to come.'

'Michael was coming on pretty strong last night. I don't want to let Squidge down.'

'You won't. Look, Lia. You're not like Ollie. He's a player. You're not. You're straight. Squidge knows that.'

'I don't know . . .'

Cat sighed, then she grinned. 'You have to come. For one thing, you have to take photos of it all for Squidge. It sounds like it's going to be such a great night and he'd never forgive you if you missed it. Don't worry. I'll look after you. I'll make sure that you never get left alone with Michael for one thing.'

'I don't know . . . I . . .'

Cat was up and at the wardrobe where she pulled out my white jeans and a top. 'You're coming. You have to. For Squidge. You promised that you'd be his eyes while you're here. So come on. I won't take no for an answer.'

The coach turned off the main road, drove down bumpy country roads then dropped us off in a field where it seemed like half the tourists (if not all) from Marrakech were disembarking. By now, it was dark except for the headlights of taxis and coaches and, up above, the stars in the sky.

'This might be a really naff touristy-type event,' I said as we made our way through the fumes from the coaches towards a gate in a high wall. 'So don't get your hopes up.'

A crowd of people were jostling their way in and I was beginning to wish that I'd stayed back at the hotel as I get claustrophobic when there are too many people around. I took a few shots and then looked for the girls. Becca, Cat, Rhiannon and Star were with me one moment and then I couldn't see them amidst all the people pushing to get in. I looked around, in front, behind, but there was no sign of them. I was being moved along by the sheer weight of the crowd and put away the camera in case it got crushed. All of a sudden, Michael was beside me and he took my hand and pulled me forward.

'Hang on to me,' he said and pulled me through the door.

It was as if we'd stepped through the looking glass like Alice in the Lewis Carroll books. The crowd dispersed and we were in another world. A magic world of light and perfume and fantasy.

Standing in front of us were two rows of beautiful white horses, on which sat Berber tribesmen with their guns making an arch for the arriving tourists to walk through. At the end of the arch, pretty little Moroccan girls dressed in the traditional costume beckoned us towards them. Hand in hand, Michael and I followed and when we reached the girls, they put their hands into baskets of rose petals and scattered them over us. I felt like we were a bride and groom being showered in confetti.

Our pretty guides led us through an archway into an inner courtyard. They took us past a group of traditional musicians who were playing drums and singing, then through another archway and into a huge open space as big as a football pitch which was surrounded by open tent-type rooms each containing low tables and chairs which were set for dinner. Behind the tents were high walls like those of a castle. Wonderful smells of cooking – onions, spices, garlic and rosemary – wafted through the air. It was like walking into a medieval city. A guide came over to us, took our names then led us to a large tent at the end of the field. Most of our party were already in there, seated on cushions on the floor around five or six tables. As Michael and I were among the last to arrive, we were put on a table together to the right. Luckily Cat, Becca and Jamie were also present. Cat looked at Michael then me and mouthed, 'Sorry.' I shrugged my shoulders at her. It was OK. There were so many people around that I doubted that he'd try anything.

The entertainment began almost straight away. Waiters dressed in tribal costume doubled as performers and one after the other they arrived at the flaps of the tent: dancers, snake-charmers, fire-eaters, jugglers, musicians with tambourines, bells, drums and pipes. They would perform, bow and move on to the next tent. Others returned to bring lamb, roasted vegetables, couscous, wine and mint tea.

'This is a fab night,' said Cat as she sat back against one of the cushions and grinned widely. I noticed that Jamie took her hand when she said this and she didn't pull it away. Hmm. Interesting, I thought. Ollie has competition. Good for Cat.

'Aren't you glad you came?' asked Becca.

I nodded. I was. The name 'Fantasia' for the evening was perfect as it really did feel like we had been transported into a film set depicting another era. A couple of times Michael passed me something and our hands touched and he seemed to be watching me with the same intensity as he had on the plane. I would glance at him and smile. I hoped he got the message. Nothing was going to happen.

After supper, we were all invited to go and sit on the raised concrete benches around the edges of the field in the middle of the arena. When everyone was seated, lights were turned off in the area and flares at the back of the field blazed brightly, lighting up the sky. Music blasted out of speakers at each end, filling the night with the most glorious sounds.

'It's *Carmina Burana*,' said Dad, coming up behind me. 'One of my favourite pieces of music.'

As the music burst forth, so did the sound of horses' hooves, and suddenly spotlights flooded the field, lighting up the most amazing spectacle. Horses and their riders in full tribal costume were charging down the field at full pelt. As they rode, they went into a show of acrobatics, swinging over and up on the horse's back, all the time riding so fast it took your breath away to watch them. And then they rode four, five, six to a horse. After the acrobatics, another group of horsemen charged forward, hollering and shaking guns. As they reached the end of the field, they all fired their rifles into the sky, causing Becca to almost jump out of her skin. I tried to get it on camera but the experience was so amazing that after a while I put it down to watch.

After the horse show, the lights dimmed and a softer light came on along with a troupe of belly dancers shimmering their way across the field. Up in the sky, a magic carpet appeared to fly across the field carrying a prince and his princess.

And then suddenly it was over. The lights went off and we were left standing, looking at the full moon and stars.

At least I thought it was over. With an almighty roar,

the sky exploded with the blaze of hundreds of fireworks. All faces turned to the sky and, as I turned mine, I felt hands slip around my waist from behind me.

It was Michael.

As the sky blazed bright and music blasted out of speakers, Michael turned me round to face him, cupped my chin in one of his hands, slipped his hand round the back of my head and pulled me to him.

And then he kissed me on the lips.

Playboy of the Western World

11

OLLIE CORNERED ME the moment I got back to the hotel. He reeked of beer.

'So what's going on with Cat and Jamie?' he asked grumpily.

'Dunno. Ask Jamie. He's your friend.'

Ollie grunted. 'Humph. Then I'll look like a real prat. Best mate gets off with my girlfriend.'

'Your girlfriend? Er . . . reality check. Since when?'

'I've always liked Cat. You know that.'

'And a million others. Like, what about that girl from London?'

'I never lied about what I was like.'

'That's true. So it's your own fault then,' I said. 'It's your choice to be the playboy of the western world. I mean, how many times have you told Cat that you like her but aren't into commitment.'

'It's true. I'm not into commitment. And neither should Cat be. You miss out on too much if you tie yourself down at our age. And that goes for you too. You know Michael fancies you, don't you?'

'Does he?' I asked, hoping that I looked cooler than I felt.

'Yeah. But you've only got eyes for that Squidge. Cat used to go out with Squidge, you know. You should go out with more boys. Live a little. You don't have to get tied down so young. I mean, you're only . . . what are you?'

'Fourteen. Are you drunk?'

'Evewee-bodee should just have a good time. So where is Cat?'

I laughed. 'Ollie, the "I'm not into commitment" line doesn't just apply to Ollie Axford, you know. Maybe she's listened to what you had to say and she's following your advice and hanging out with Jamie because of it.'

A look of confusion flashed across his face. 'Uh? But I meant that *she* shouldn't expect *me* to be committed to her. Not that I thought she should play the field. Huh.'

'Poor Ollie. You expected her to just sit around until you happened to glance her way. She has a life, you know.'

'Yeah. Hmpff . . .' said Ollie. He flounced off, then

turned back. 'She wants *me*, you know . . .' he slurred. 'She really wants me . . .'

He zig-zagged across the corridor and I hoped he had the good sense to go straight to bed as Ollie doesn't drink a lot normally. At least he didn't ask any awkward questions about Michael, I thought, but then knowing Ollie and how self-absorbed he can be sometimes, he probably never even noticed that his mate had kissed his sister under his nose.

I carried on into my room, checked my mobile in case there were any messages from Squidge (there weren't), fell into bed and was asleep in seconds.

Next thing I knew, someone was gently shaking me awake.

'Lia, Lia . . .'

It was Cat. I sat up and rubbed my eyes. 'Wha—'

She sat on the end of my bed. 'So?' she asked.

Becca appeared behind her then went round to sit on the other side. 'Yeah. So?' she asked.

I knew it had been too good to last. I might have been able to avoid questions from my brother but I should have known better than to think my two mates wouldn't interrogate me.

'And *so* to you two as well,' I replied. 'Where do you think you've been? I've been in bed for ages.'

'What happened with Michael?' asked Becca. 'We saw you ki–'

'Not really . . .'

'Looked that way to me,' said Becca. 'I've been dying to get back here and ask you but Henry wanted to have an . . . um . . . a late-night walk.'

'And what's your excuse, Cat?' I asked.

'You sound like my dad,' she said with a grin. 'Er. Jamie. Moonlight walk. You know how it is.'

'Yeah and so does Ollie. He's not very happy. He cornered me on the way in and he was well grumpy.'

Cat shrugged. 'Ollie has made it very clear in the past that he likes to be a free agent. Two can play at that game. Actually, no. I'm not playing a game. I like Jamie. He's great company and, as Ollie keeps saying, we're not in a serious relationship so that means that I'm a free agent too. Besides, Jamie's a good snogger.'

'Never mind Ollie and Jamie,' said Becca. 'What about Michael? What about Squidge?'

'Start with Michael,' said Cat. 'He got you on your own again. I'm sorry I wasn't more of a chaperone at the Fantasia but it was all so . . .'

'Not your fault,' I interrupted. 'Other things to occupy you. So, um, yeah, Michael. He's a great guy and he gave me some really good advice about my confusion about what I want to do when I leave school.'

'Advice? Confusion?' blurted Becca. 'When was this?'

'On the coach,' I said. 'He gave me some advice on the coach on the way back.'

'No. The confusion? What confusion?' asked Becca, who was starting to look really confused herself.

'Mine. About what I'm going to do with my life.'

'Your life? Duh? No. Go back a bit,' said Becca. 'Never mind advice. What about the snogging?'

'But he did give me advice,' I said. 'He said that if I want to be a vet, I should go and do a few weeks' work experience in a clinic. I'll soon find out if I'm suited or not. Same with any job. Ask around. Then go and try it out.'

'Mmm, sound advice,' said Cat, settling in on the end of the bed so I threw her one of my pillows. 'What does he want to do?'

'Journalist. But at first he wanted to be a doctor. He was so funny about it. Said he thought it would be all glam, swanning about in a white coat having people look up to him. Said the reality is waaay different. No sleep, hard work and no time off.'

'So he wanted to be a doctor so he could pose?' asked Cat.

'Sort of,' I said.

I knew we were winding Becca up like mad as she was sitting on her side of the bed watching Cat and me like she was watching a tennis ball go back and forth at a tennis match. I knew she was going to burst at any moment.

'Well, I'm really glad he found out that it wasn't for him before it was too late,' said Cat. 'Can you imagine someone going in with a pain or illness and he'd be there saying, OK, but just a minute, let me fix my hair! And lie down over there but make sure when you look up, you get my good profile . . .'

We started laughing and Becca finally cracked. 'It's *two* in the morning and you two are sitting here discussing a boy's career prospects! Are you *insane*? You've clearly both been drinking too much of that mint tea. Listen. Michael. Last seen snogging you at the firework display? And then sitting in the back of the coach as cosy as anything on the way back? That's what I want to hear about. Not if he's going to star in *ER* or not, Lia. *Details. Please.* I feel like I've missed an episode of my favourite soap and suddenly the plot's moved on and I don't know what's happening.' She rolled on to her side and groaned. 'Put me out of my misery.'

'Not that much happened really. OK, here's the story. For the briefest, briefest second when Michael kissed me, I responded. Only for a nanosecond. It soon became clear that much as I have fancied him in the past, it wasn't the same as kissing Squidge, so I pulled back. When he asked what the matter was, I told him the truth. I explained that there we were under the stars. And miles away was Squidge under the same stars but in hospital. Different countries but same stars.'

'Ahhh, that's so romantic,' said Becca.

'And I couldn't be disloyal to him,' I continued. 'We have something really special and I didn't want to cheat on him.'

'How did Michael take that?' asked Cat.

'He was quiet for a while and at first I thought he was going to be mad at me but then he smiled and said, Good for you, Lia. He said he understood and even admired me for it. He said that Squidge is a really lucky man and he wished he could find someone who would be as true to him in the circumstances we've been in. I guess he meant here. I mean all the fabulous locations we've been in during the last couple of days. I knew what he meant. It hasn't been easy at times but in a way it's all served to make me realise how strong my feelings for Squidge really are.'

'Wow,' said Becca. 'You and Squidge are soulmates.'

It had been amazing with Michael. And sad, in a way. I replayed the last moments in my head. I didn't want to tell

Cat and Becca everything that he said because I felt that it was private between me and him. Michael had put his hand on my shoulder and looked into my eyes. 'Me and you?' he'd said. 'Bad timing, I suppose. I should have nabbed you when you were nine and really into me . . .'

'When I was nine?' I'd said. 'So you *knew* I had a crush on you? Oh God, *nooooo*. How embarrassing.'

'Nah. You were sweet. Really sweet. And then when I saw you again last year. All grown up. Remember when I came down with Usha? Umph. She gave me such a hard time about you but I swore to her that nothing had ever happened. But . . . ah well. Maybe some day, hey? A few years down the line?'

'You never know.'

Michael had leaned over and kissed me on the cheek. 'Later.'

I'd taken his hand and squeezed it. 'Later.'

Cat and Becca got up to get ready for bed when there was a noise at the door. It sounded as though someone had fallen over in the corridor outside our room. Becca got up to see what or who it was and, when she opened the door, there on his knees with his hair all squiffy was Ollie.

'Where Ca–?' he slurred.

Cat quickly ducked down behind the bed.

'Oh,' said Becca. 'She's in bed. And I suggest that's where you go to.'

'She wants me, you know,' he said with his lopsided grin.

'Have you been drinking?' asked Becca, going into her prefect act.

'Yeah . . . no . . . a liryl . . .'

'You're a very bad boy, Ollie Axford. Now go to bed.'

'OK buh . . . Cat . . . She wants me, you know . . .'

Cat and I were having a hard time not laughing out loud as Ollie did sound funny.

'Yeah. Sure,' said Becca. 'I know. Cat wants you. But not now. Now go to bed.'

'She gus, you know.'

'Off you go now, Ollie. Good boy.'

Ollie sat back on his heels. 'Do you want me?' he asked.

'Sure. Everyone wants you, Ollie. Now go to bed.'

'Want to come too?'

It was at this point that I decided that maybe Becca needed help.

'You stay here,' I whispered to Cat then went out into the corridor to find that by now Ollie had flopped over on his side and had curled up ready to sleep in the corridor.

'Evewee wants me . . .' he murmured then stuck his thumb in his mouth like a baby.

'Playboy of the western world,' I said.

'Get your camera,' whispered Becca.

I tiptoed back into the room, found the camera and quickly snapped a shot. 'Be great blackmail material,' I laughed.

'Yeah,' whispered Becca. 'We could post it on the Internet with a note saying, *Does anybody recognise this boy?*'

Ollie began to stir then reached for my ankles. 'Cat . . .'

I nodded at Becca and she went to his front and grabbed one of his wrists. I got the other and between us we managed to drag him back to the boys' room, where we knocked then left him propped up against the door like a puppet without its strings.

Essaouira

12

'HI, SQUIDGE. THIS IS LIA AGAIN,' I said into my mobile. 'Please call as soon as you can. We all miss you like crazy and wish you were here. Hope you're feeling better and everyone sends their love.'

'He must still be in the hospital,' said Cat from across the table, where she was spreading a croissant with apricot jam. 'Otherwise he would have called.'

'And he can't hobble outside to use his mobile,' said Becca as she sipped her fresh orange juice, 'not with a broken leg.'

'I guess,' I agreed. But inside I felt that something was wrong. I was about to call Squidge's parents when Mum arrived at our table.

'Hi, Mum. Where is everyone this morning?' I asked as

I indicated the half-empty dining room.

She laughed. 'Some are hung over from last night so still in bed. Some have already gone off on the mountain trip. And the others are getting ready for Essaouira.'

'Ollie?'

'Dead to the world,' said Mum. 'Serves him right too. Stupid boy.'

'Are you mad with him?'

Mum shrugged. 'He'll learn the hard way. He is almost eighteen, after all,' she said. 'Anyway, seems he wasn't the only one who had a few too many last night. Jamie and Henry don't seem to be quite with it this morning either.'

'But I thought the boys were going up to the mountains?'

Mum shook her head. 'The guide left over an hour ago with the guests who were up in time for that trip. No, I think Ollie and Henry and Jamie won't be going any further than their bedroom this morning.'

'And Michael?'

'He's fine. He's coming to Essaouira with us. He's such a nice boy, don't you think?'

'Oh not you too, Mum.'

'Not me too what?'

'Michael. Just about every member of my family has hinted that Michael and I should go out or something. You,

Ollie, Dad. I'm with Squidge. Sometimes I think you don't take that seriously.'

Mum put her hand on my arm. 'Yes we do. Squidge is a nice boy too and I wasn't insinuating anything about Michael, not really. Just . . . well, you're still young, Lia, with a whole world of boys to go out with . . .'

'I quite agree,' said Becca. 'The more the merrier.'

It was Cat who came to my defence. 'Yes, but Lia and Squidge have something special,' she said.

At that moment, Michael came in and waved from the other side of the dining room. I waved back. I hoped that it would be OK if we spent the day together. Although the air had been cleared between us after our conversation last night, I still wasn't sure that I would ever be totally relaxed with him. One thing I had realised though and that was that Squidge had been right. Michael and I were from the same type of background and we were very alike. And *that* was why we would never work as a couple. We were too alike. Two peas in a pod. Boring. Squidge and I were like chalk and cheese. He was outgoing. I was quiet. We were a classic case of opposites attract. Anyway, I thought, it was the last day of the trip and this evening I'd be back with Squidge and any dangerous encounters with Michael Bradley in romantic settings would be well behind me.

We set out for the seaside half an hour later and the journey took almost two hours. Part of me would have liked to have stayed in Marrakech but I knew that Squidge had particularly wanted to see Essaouira as it had been used as a location in a number of movies, the most famous being *Othello*, *Kingdom of Heaven*, *Troy* and *Alexander*. I had to go for Squidge and take what pictures I could for him.

We had a great day there. After the hustle bustle of Marrakech, it provided the perfect contrast. Essaouira was a gentler place with a cooler climate due to the breeze that blew in from the Atlantic and through the warren of lanes and alleyways inside the walled town. Outside the walls was a pretty fishing port and to the left a long wide sandy beach. After a fab lunch of fresh fish at a café on the beach, we walked by the sea and then explored the souks and stalls, while Dad looked around to see if he recognised any of it from his childhood. I needn't have worried about Michael being with us. He was totally cool. He chatted away to Mum and Dad and was warm and friendly with me but had stopped giving me the intense stares like he had earlier on the trip. I think he'd accepted that nothing was going to happen between us.

I particularly loved the town as everywhere there were cats and kittens. On every corner, under tables, under chairs and basking in the sun, it seemed that there were as many of them as people! And it seemed as if they were well looked after as more than once we saw people putting out bits of fish for the kittens to come and munch on.

'That's just what I feel like doing,' said Mum as we saw one white and ginger cat lying on its back on a white wall.

Mid-afternoon we went up to the fort area to explore and as the others went off to look at some of the pottery on sale in one of the arches there, I took some photos of the row of ancient cannons lined up on the castle wall. I was amazed that so many of them had survived. I sat on the wall next to one of the cannons and pulled out my mobile to see if there were any messages. There was a text from Ollie: %*@:-(SORRY (meaning 'I am hungover with a headache'), but nothing from Squidge. I decided I'd to call his home number and see if I could find out anything from his mum.

Mrs Squires picked up immediately. 'Lia! That you? Are you home?'

'No, I'm still in Morocco.'

'No! Amazing. You're calling from Morocco?'

'Yes. I was wondering how Squidge is?'

'Oh, a lot better since he got home. He was going out of his mind with boredom being cooped up in the hospital . . .'

'He's home? But . . . when?'

'We brought him back yesterday, late afternoon.'

'Can I speak to him?'

'Sure. I'll take the phone in to him.'

The line went quiet for a few minutes and then Mrs Squires came back on. 'Er . . . Lia, love. He says he'll talk to you when you're back.'

'But why won't he talk to me now?'

'He's in the downstairs cloakroom. He'll probably call you when he's out.'

'Oh. OK. But he is all right?' I asked.

'Oh yes. He's fine,' said Mrs Squires. 'Don't you worry yourself. Enjoy the rest of your holiday.'

After I'd put the phone down, I felt puzzled. Why hadn't Squidge called yesterday as soon as he'd got out of hospital? I'd left enough messages asking him to let me know the moment they released him. I knew that mobiles weren't allowed in the hospital and no way would they let him call Morocco from the ward phone but if he was home, he could have. And I could have sent him photos on my phone. He'd have loved the unspoilt look of Essaouira; it was a film director's dream of a location and, having been there, I could understand why it had been used in so many movies. Squidge knew I had my photo phone with me. Why didn't he want to see where I was? A horrible feeling hit my stomach and even though the sun was beating down, I felt a shiver of cold. The signs weren't good. Something had happened.

Later, as we drove back into Marrakech, all I could think about was getting home then getting down to Cawsand village to see Squidge. I checked my mobile every five minutes and still he hadn't called me back. Why not? He'd had days in bed, maybe that was it. Days to think about things. About us. He'd had space to think about what he wants and where he's going next. Maybe he'd realised that he's bored with me. Wants to move on. He's always saying that he wants new experiences. He has to have them if he's going to be a good film director. Maybe he's realised that I have nothing more to offer him and that he could do better. He could find himself a girl with talents and ambitions to match his. Someone who would entertain him. Maybe he'd been thinking like Mum, and also thought that we were too young to be tied down when there was a whole world of other girls he could be dating. I felt so frustrated being so far away from him. In another time zone, in another country. Not knowing what he was thinking.

As we approached the hotel, Ollie and Jamie were coming towards us along the side of the narrow lane. Both of them spotted Cat in the back and as the car slowed down, Ollie put on a tragic expression, spread his arms out and mock threw himself on to the bonnet. And then Cat started laughing. Unseen by Ollie, Jamie was posing behind him like a call girl. He pursed his lips, leaned on one hip, pulled the trouser leg on his left leg up to reveal his ankle, then he wiggled his hips, batted his eyelashes at our baffled driver and stuck his thumb out as though he was trying to hitch a lift.

Cat and Becca burst out laughing and Ollie looked mystified as to why they'd been distracted from his performance and why they were cracking up. For a moment, I felt sorry for my gorgeous brother. He might be a babe magnet and exceptionally good-looking but when a boy can make you laugh like Jamie could, boys like Ollie didn't get a look in. I wondered if Ollie ever felt like I did. Not enough to offer. I glanced back at them as the car drove on. No. I doubted that Ollie ever felt that way.

As soon as we were out of the car, it was up to our rooms, pack our bags, head for the plane and it was bye-bye Morocco.

An hour later, we were up in the sky and heading home. It had been a stunning trip and everyone said they'd had the time of their lives. Mum, Dad, Cat, Becca, Meena. Everyone had loved it and was sorry to leave Marrakech.

It seemed that it was only me who couldn't wait to get back.

At the airport back in the UK, a people carrier was waiting for us on the runway and Cat, Becca and I took the back seat while Mum and Dad sat in the middle and Meena in the front with the driver.

As soon as we were on our way, I tried to call Squidge's mobile again.

His phone was still switched off.

His silence was killing me.

'Still can't get through?' asked Becca.

I shook my head.

'Try the landline,' said Cat. 'His mum is bound to be there.'

I dialled the number and a few moments later Mrs Squires picked up. I hope she doesn't mind me calling all the time, I thought as I asked how he was *again*.

'We've set up a bed for him in the front room,' said Mrs Squires. 'So that he doesn't have to hobble up and down the stairs. Makes life easier all round. I'll take the phone in. Back now, are you?'

'Just landed,' I said. 'I tried his mobile but it's still switched off. So he's doing OK?'

'Yes. Fine. Bit tired. Hold on a sec.'

I held my breath and prayed that he'd take my call this time. As I waited, I couldn't help but feel anxious. Don't be mad, I thought, this is Squidge. Your boyfriend. What is there to be anxious about?

A moment later, I heard Squidge's voice on the other end of the line and I sighed with relief.

'Hello.'

'Hey, Squidge,' I said. 'It's me. Lia.'

'Oh. Hi. You're back.'

'Yeah. Just now. I called as soon as I could.'

'Hey, you didn't need to do that. How was it?'

'Brilliant. I tried to call you but your mobile's switched off.'

'I know. I kept leaving it somewhere awkward and then it would ring and it was such an almighty effort getting up to get to it that I switched it off.'

'I wanted to come and see you but Mum says we'll be back too late. Probably not until gone eleven.'

'Well, it's not like I'm going anywhere far for the next week or so.'

'I'll come after school tomorrow. I've got loads of photos to show you.'

'Oh OK. Cool. Thanks.'

It was hard to tell without seeing his face but he didn't

sound very excited about seeing the photos nor too enthusiastic about me going round there.

'Would you . . . er . . . you do want visitors, don't you?'

'God, yes. *Yeah.* Course I do. I've been going out of my mind with boredom and it feels like I've been like this for ages, much longer than a week. So yeah be great to see you all and hear all about it. I bet Cat and Becca loved it, hey?'

See us all? Becca and Cat? I wasn't imagining it. He was being distant with me. It began to feel more and more urgent that I got round there as soon as possible.

'Yeah, they loved it. OK, tomorrow then,' I said.

'Sure. No rush. I've got a bunch of DVDs to watch if you have things to do.'

'Which ones?'

'*Kill Bill.*'

'One or Two?'

'Both. Not a lot else I can do except revision for my GCSEs and then sit and watch DVDs. Dad got me a load out of the shop.'

'And we've got loads up at the house. I can bring them down tomorrow.'

'OK. Thanks.'

'Want me to stay and watch with you tomorrow night?'

'Yeah. Course, if you like, but I'm halfway into number

one and you'll be tired after your journey. So don't worry if you can't.'

I can take a hint, I thought. He doesn't want me there. He's moved on and I'm history.

'OK. See you tomorrow then,' I said.

See you tomorrow then, I thought. Hah. If only I could say what I felt which was . . . Squidge, what's going on? Do you still like me? Are we OK? Have you gone off me? But I knew I couldn't. Not only because I was in a people carrier with six other people but also because the sensible part of me knew that over the phone is no place to have that kind of conversation. And another part of me knew that it would make me sound like a desperate saddo and there's nothing more guaranteed to put a boy off than a girl going all intense and emotional on him.

'Yeah. See you,' said Squidge.

I clicked my phone shut and stared out of the car window into the dark night. I felt rotten and speaking to him had only made my feeling of panic get worse.

Cat put her hand on my arm. 'What's up? Is he OK?'

I nodded and filled her and Becca in on my phone call.

'I think he wants to finish with me,' I whispered so that Mum and Dad couldn't hear. 'I think it's over.'

'No,' said Cat. 'I don't. I think you're being oversensitive.'

'You think?'

'Yeah. Phone calls can be deceptive. It's easier to know what's going on when you can see someone's eyes. Wait until you see him tomorrow.'

'I guess . . . just . . . I don't know. I've got a feeling that he's gone off me.'

'Never,' said Cat. 'Squidge adores you. You're being paranoid.'

'It's amazing,' said Becca, 'because when I first got to know you, I thought you were the girl who had everything because . . . well . . . you do. The whole package. But you're the least confident person I have ever met. I don't know why. And as Cat said, Squidge clearly adores you.'

'He doesn't want me to stay and watch the movie with him tomorrow . . .'

'Ah, but that might be you being oversensitive again,' said Cat. 'Don't forget that I've known Squidge a lot longer than you and two things I can guarantee: one – that he hates being dependent on people and is probably feeling grumpy about it, and two – that he's thinking about you. He's one of the most thoughtful people I know, in fact, *you* know that he is, Lia. It could well have been that he does want you to stay but knows that you will be tired after

133

school tomorrow. I know I am now. I'm knackered and I'm going to sleep like a log tonight.'

'Me, too,' said Becca and she laid her head on Cat's shoulder and promptly fell asleep. I spent the rest of the journey staring out into the night and replaying and replaying my conversation with Squidge in my head.

As soon as we got home, it was up to bed.

I felt I was being woken two seconds after I'd closed my eyes, but no, it was morning, Monday and back to school.

I tried my best to focus on my lessons and not think about the fact that Squidge was just down the road. It was strange to think that he was so close and yet he felt as far away as he had when I was in Morocco.

'Let's find Mac,' said Becca in the lunch break. 'I bet he'll want to know how it all went.'

'Yeah, and maybe he's seen Squidge and knows how he is,' said Cat.

We found Mac in the art room and his face lit up when he saw us.

'Hey, it's the golden girls,' he said when we walked in. 'How did it go?'

'Excellent,' said Becca as I got the digital camera out to show him the photos.

'I told my dad that I missed out,' he said as we showed him the pics of the roof terrace party. 'And he promised that if I get good results in my GCSEs then he will take me to Morocco himself. So I might not have to miss out after all. Still, I would have given anything to have been there with you lot.'

'Do you think that's what's the matter with Squidge?' asked Becca. 'He's fed up because he missed out on the trip. Lia said he was a bit cool with her on the phone last night.'

'Really? I saw him yesterday and he was OK.'

'He wasn't when I spoke to him,' I said. 'And he hasn't texted or called today. Did he say anything? Have I done something?'

'Not that he mentioned to me.'

'Well, has anything happened while we were gone?'

'Not that I know of,' said Mac. 'Not a lot that Squidge could get up to with a broken leg and collarbone, although he did mention something about a nurse. A naughty nurse . . .' Then he laughed. 'Only teasing, Lia. No nurse. Least, not that I know of. I shouldn't worry. When I think about it, I guess he has been a bit low but who can blame him, cooped up all week? You know Squidge, he hates to feel he can't get up and go.'

At that moment, my mobile bleeped that there was a message.

It was from Squidge and I braced myself for a message asking me not to go after school.

INVALID IN NEED OF SAUCY YOUNG NURSE. PLEASE COME IN UNIFORM AS SOON AS POSS AND BRING HOLIDAY PICS. PREFERABLY ALL NAKED ONES.

'Crisis over,' I said.

Invalid

13

SQUIDGE WAS THE HERO OF THE HOUR. Judging by the reception he got when he came back to school halfway through the week, anyone would have thought he'd come back from the dead or scored the winning goal in a Cup Final. Girls from Year Seven and Eight traipsed after him carrying his books. The boys from Year Eleven offered him lifts back and forth from the village and soon there was a rota organised to get him to school and back for all his GCSE exams.

'He's really popular, isn't he?' commented Becca at Friday lunchtime as we sat in the sun on a wall at the back of the playground.

'Yeah, and he's lapping this up,' said Cat as she watched Squidge on the other side of the playground get stopped by some kid who wanted to sign his plaster cast. 'I think just about everyone in the school has signed his leg. He's got rock star status like your dad, Lia.'

Yeah, I thought. And is hard to get alone. Squidge and I hadn't had any time by ourselves since I'd got back from Morocco. Whenever I went to visit, one of his thousand relatives were there and they wanted to see the Morocco pictures too. Squidge had put the whole trip on to his computer and was happy to show everyone – as if he had actually been there himself. There was so much I wanted to talk to him about. Niggling doubts and fears that he had grown tired of me, my growing paranoia. I just wanted some time when he could reassure me that we were still an item.

He finally reached us, put his rucksack down, gave his crutches to Cat, then slowly manoeuvred himself against the wall.

'So what's everyone going to wear for the midsummer's night party?' he asked.

'Ohmigod, I'd completely forgotten about that,' said Becca. 'I still haven't recovered from Morocco.'

'Well, you'd better get a move on,' said Squidge. 'It's a week on Saturday.'

'I wish I could forget about it,' I said. 'Mum went

straight into overdrive as soon as we got home from Morocco. All that fuss about not wanting a party for her birthday and now there's no stopping her.'

'Yeah, but it's different this time,' said Cat. 'It's not for her birthday. I had a chat to her about it when we were in Marrakech. It's like it's one thing doing parties for someone else but on your own birthday, you want to be princess for a day and have someone else do everything for you.'

Cat knew only too well about organising parties too. As her mum died when she was nine, sometimes she ends up acting like a replacement mum to her younger brothers and sister. She's the one who makes them their birthday cakes and makes sure they have presents and cards on the day. I made a mental note to really spoil Cat on her next birthday and make sure she was princess for a day.

'Well, Mum was certainly treated like royalty for a day in Morocco,' I said. 'And she loved it. But now, she's organising a marquee, ordering food, flowers . . .'

'Dress as a character from the play, the invite says,' said Squidge. 'So. Who shall we go as?'

'Go as? I have no idea. I don't know the story of *A Midsummer Night's Dream*,' said Becca. 'Who wrote it? It was Charles Dickens or Shakespeare, wasn't it? One of them?'

'Shakespeare,' said Squidge. 'A *Midsummer Night's Dream* was written about 1594–95 and I can tell you all you need to know about it because it's one of the plays we're doing for GCSE English. In fact, if you like, come over to our house tonight. I can run through the story and the characters with you. It will help me with my revision. In fact, I think I've got a DVD of it somewhere. It's a great version. Michelle Pfeiffer as Titania, Rupert Everett as Oberon and Kevin Kline as the ass.'

Becca rolled her eyes. 'The ass? Titania? Oberwho? Like, duh? I have no idea what or who you're talking about.'

'It's a great story,' said Cat. 'You'll like it, Becca. It's all about love and relationships getting mixed up. There's a bad . . . well, maybe not bad, a naughty fairy in it called Puck and he goes round putting a magic potion in people's eyes when they're asleep so that they fall in love with the first person they see when they wake up. He puts some in Titania's eyes – she's the Queen of the Fairies – and when she wakes up, she sees an ass and falls in love with him . . .'

'Sounds like the story of my life,' said Becca. 'I think I'll go as her.'

'No way is it the story of your life,' said Cat. 'Henry was nice. And so was Mac. How can you say that?'

Becca laughed. 'Maybe just feels like that sometimes. Boys. They're all stupid.'

'Thanks a bunch,' said Squidge.

'OK. *Most* boys are stupid,' said Becca. 'I think I'll go into the library and see if they have the play in there. Want to come, Cat?'

'Sure,' said Cat and she slid off the wall to go with her.

As soon as they'd gone, Squidge pointed at his rucksack. 'Hey, in there, I got something for you. Front pocket.'

I bent over and found an envelope.

'Pics of your trip,' said Squidge as I pulled the envelope out. 'I've been playing around with them in Photoshop and printed some out.'

I pulled the photos out and flicked through.

He'd zoomed in on some of the shots I'd taken and blown them up.

'Wow, these are amazing, Squidge.'

'Yeah, well, you did a good job,' he said and pointed to one of my mum. 'I thought your mum would like that. I've airbrushed out all her wrinkles, not that she has many.'

I continued shuffling the photos and we came to one of Ollie, Jamie, Henry and Michael. Apart from Michael, they were laughing at something off to the right of the camera.

In contrast, Michael was looking straight at me with the expression that he'd had on the plane and on the roof terrace and at Fantasia. An intense expression like he'd seen something that he wanted. Badly.

'That's that Michael guy, isn't it?' asked Squidge.

I shuffled the photo to the bottom of the pile. 'Yeah. And Jamie and Henry.'

I'd already filled him in on all the gossip: What was happening with Cat and Ollie and Jamie. And how Henry had taken a shine to Becca. How Ollie had got the hump as he wasn't the man of the moment any more. I purposely hadn't said anything about Michael, although he was there in a lot of the photographs. I didn't want to draw any attention to him.

'You didn't say much about how he was on the trip,' Squidge persisted.

I nodded. 'Not much to say. He hung out with Ollie mainly.'

'Did he enjoy the trip?'

'Yeah. Think so.'

'Did he get off with anyone?'

'Don't think so.'

'Maybe he's still with that lovely Indian girl?'

I was starting to feel uncomfortable. Why was Squidge

interrogating me? I knew I'd have to be really careful what I said and how I said it because, as he knew, I'm a lousy liar. 'No. They've split up.'

I carried on sifting through the prints with Squidge looking over my shoulder. When I'd finished, he took them and sifted through again until he reached the shot with Michael watching me. 'He's looking right at you as you're taking the shots. Watching you. I think he fancies you. Truth, Lia. Was there . . . *is* there something between you and this guy?'

The question I'd been dreading. Oh God, I thought as I felt my insides shrink. What can I say? What should I say? The longer I hesitated, the more it appeared that I had something to hide. I took a deep breath and decided to tell Squidge the truth.

'No. Truth. There used to be. At least on my side. I used to have a crush on him. Ages ago. But it never came to anything because he always saw me as Ollie's kid sister. A kid.'

Squidge kept his eyes on the photo. 'And what about now? He's not looking at you like he's looking at a kid.'

'I told him straight off that I'm going out with you. I don't want anyone else. I don't want Michael. I want you. That's the truth.'

Squidge turned, took my hand and looked deep into my eyes.

'Are you sure, Lia? Are you really sure? Because I would hate to hold you back. This Michael, he's . . . he's the kind of guy that you deserve. He's from your world . . .'

'My world! What world? I live in the same world as you do.'

Squidge laughed. 'Yeah, right. Get real, Lia. We might go to the same school but we do not inhabit the same planet when we go home.'

'Yes we do. We *do*. We sleep. We do our homework. We hang out with our mates. What are you trying to say, Squidge?'

Squidge sighed. 'Oh, I don't know. I don't. Sorry. Just . . . I need to know. Did something happen between you and this Michael guy?'

I shook my head. '*No. Truth*. And I told him from the start that I was with you and just because he was single now, didn't mean that I was available too.'

'Ah. So he *did* make a play for you?'

'Er . . . yeah. *No*. Not really. I mean nothing heavy and I told him straight . . .'

'How did he make a play for you?'

'Oh Squidge . . . you know, looks . . . sitting next to me.

Honestly, Squidge, there is nothing between us. And you know what? Him being there and you not, it made me realise how special it is between us. And it *is,* isn't it?'

Squidge was quiet for a few moments. 'Yeah. *Really* special. Just sometimes . . . I wish . . . well, I wish I had more. I wish I could offer you more. I wish my life wasn't so ordinary.'

'You? But you're Captain Popular around here. You're not ordinary. Don't you see that? Everyone wants to be with you.'

'Yeah but . . . I ride a push-bike. I bet Michael has some new state-of-the-art car. I live in a back street in the village. You live in a mansion and I bet Michael lives somewhere trendy and posh in London. Somewhere someone like you belongs. I bet he could take you places . . .'

'Squidge, you don't get it, do you? I don't want that. If I want to ride in a fancy car, I can. My dad's or my mum's or Ollie's or Star's. Yeah, I live in a great place, but those things don't make me happy. It's having friends and people I like and love to hang out with that makes me happy. OK, so yeah, I don't think I'd like to be poor but I tell you, when I first came down here, I was so lonely. Up there in our gorgeous house with our gorgeous things and all I wanted was someone to talk to and have a laugh with. Anyway, I don't see you in those terms, rich or poor. I see you as someone I love spending time with. Love hanging out with. You make me laugh. And who else could have shown me all the great places down here? The beaches no one else knows about? The best views? The walks?'

'Anybody who's lived down here.'

I punched him. 'No. You know all the best places. The secret places. Listen, if anyone's ordinary around here, it's me. OK, the trappings of my life are exceptional, my rock-star family, where we live . . . but me? I'm ordinary. I really am. You want to know the truth? In Morocco, I was worried out of my mind that you might be getting bored of me. All that time to lie and think in the hospital and you'd have realised it too. When you didn't return my calls, I thought I was going to go crazy. And then when I got back and you were so cool with me on the phone, remember?'

'It was all the painkillers and antibiotics. I got a chest infection in the hospital so they were pumping me full of all sorts of stuff. I wasn't being cool. I was just out of it for a while.'

'And why didn't you answer your mobile?'

'I told you. At first, it was going off all the time and I couldn't get up and answer it because of my leg and so I thought, oh, I'll put it on voice mail and then I forgot where I'd put it and couldn't look for it, not in my state . . .'

I laughed. 'I thought you didn't want to talk to me.'

Squidge laughed. 'And I was going crazy imagining you away with Mr Flash Gorgeous and that the time away would give you space to realise that I'm not good enough for you.'

I put my arms round him and gave him a big hug.

'Oooouch,' he winced. 'Careful.'

'Oh! Sorry. But . . . what a pair we are, hey? Both worried about the same thing. So you don't want to dump me?'

'Dump you! Never,' said Squidge. 'And you don't want to dump me?'

'Never.'

'I bet your dad would like it. I bet your dad wishes you were with a boy like Michael.'

'No way. I think all he cares about is that I'm happy. And you make me happy.'

He leaned over and kissed my forehead. 'And you make me happy.'

Neither of us had noticed that Mac had come up beside us and had been listening.

'I think I'm going to throw up,' he said. 'You two are like major vomitous.'

Way to Go, Shakespeario

'OK,' SAID SQUIDGE as Mac, Becca, Cat and I made ourselves comfortable on cushions on the floor in the front room of his house after school. 'Here's a list of the characters in *A Midsummer Night's Dream* for you to choose from.'

'Who are you going to go as?' asked Cat.

'Oh, whichever part makes me look most tall, dark and handsome,' Squidge replied.

Hmm. Which part will he pick? I wondered. And what will he be like when he realises that Michael Bradley will be there as all Ollie's mates are coming down again? Squidge is usually Mr Friends With Everyone so would he talk to Michael or ignore him?

Mac lay back and scrutinised the paper that Squidge had handed him. 'This is brill, mate,' he said. 'Great way for us to revise. Hey, Becca, slave girl, peel me a grape.'

'Peel your own grape, mate,' said Becca. 'I'm nobody's slave girl.'

Squidge read from one of his papers. 'OK. The play is set in Athens.'

'Or in the Axfords' case, in their back garden,' said Mac.

'Tell me about it,' I groaned. 'The decorators have been at it for days now and even though I live there, I feel like I'm in the way.'

'Theseus,' continued Squidge. 'He's the head honcho in the play, the Duke of Athens.'

'That's who Dad's going as,' I said.

'In that case, your mum should play Hippolyta – his girlfriend,' said Squidge. 'The play starts with them and they're about to have a grand do to celebrate their forthcoming wedding with lots of wonga spent, and a good time had by all.'

'Just like an Axford party,' said Becca. 'And I wouldn't call their back garden a garden, it's more like a park.'

'Anyway, along comes this guy called Egeus,' said Squidge. 'Now, he's a major control freak and wants his daughter Hermia to marry someone she doesn't want to. She actually fancies a guy called Lysander but her dad wants her to marry someone called . . . er . . .?'

'Demetrius,' said Mac. 'I remember their names because when I was little we had two goldfish called Lysander and Demetrius. I didn't know where those names came from at the time but when we did the play at school, I realised that they were a bad choice. Both the fish were female and Lysander and Demetrius are male. Anyway, sadly, Demetrius got eaten by the cat.'

'What was the cat called?' asked Becca.

'Rover.'

'Rover?'

'Yeah. We were a very mixed-up family.'

Cat rolled her eyes. 'Mad. So what next, Squidge? In the story?'

'Hermia says, "No way, José" to her dad. She doesn't want to do the arranged-wedding-type thing and really, *really* doesn't want to marry Demetrius. However, Theseus reminds her of the law that states that she has three choices. She must marry as her father wants, become a nun, or be executed.'

'No phone a friend option?' asked Becca.

'Nope.'

'Whoa. Tough call,' said Cat. 'Think I'd go for the nun of this, nun of that option if it was me. Rather that than marry someone I didn't love.'

'Enter Hermia's best mate, Helena,' Squidge continued,

'but she isn't very sympathetic. In fact, she's well pissed off with Hermia because she fancies Demetrius and thinks that Hermia was trying nick her fella. It wasn't that, though, he'd just gone off her or was giving her the runaround or something.'

'Bit of a lad, Demetrius,' said Mac. 'Has a bit of a commitment phobia.'

'Sounds like Ollie,' said Cat. 'Some things never change.'

'*The course of true love never did run smooth,*' said Mac.

'Tell me about it.'

'That's a line from the play.'

'Really?' said Cat. 'Way to go, Shakespeario.'

'Anyway,' said Squidge. 'Lysander and Hermia decide to do a runner and take off for the woods. Unbeknown to them, a bunch of fairies who have been invited to the wedding have pitched camp in there and the King and the Queen of the Fairies have had a blazing row and then . . . this is where it all gets interesting.'

'Yeah. Oberon,' said Mac, 'the King of the Fairies, is pissed off with Titania . . .'

'She's the Queen of the Fairies,' said Becca. 'I think you should go as her, Lia.'

'Yeah,' said Squidge. 'It says her character is graceful and she is very beautiful.'

'And you should go as Hermia, Cat,' said Mac. 'She's the grounded, sensible one.'

Cat pulled a face. 'Ooo, she sounds like fun. Not.'

'What about me?' asked Becca.

'Oh, Helena, definitely. She's the flighty, dippy one,' said Squidge.

Becca pouted. 'Thanks for nothing.'

'Well, that's for saying all boys are stupid the other day,' said Squidge.

'You better watch it or I'll break your other leg,' said Becca.

'Now, play nicely, children,' said Cat. 'Or you'll be sent to bed without any supper. So who else is in this? Parts for you guys?'

'Well, there's Lysander and Demetrius, of course,' said Mac. 'Plus all the artisans. Bottom, Quince, Snug, Starveling and Flute. BQSSF. That's how I try to remember names for the exams. Initials. Have you noticed all the girls' names in the play so far start with H? Helena, Hermia, Hypowhatshername – the Duke's bird. Makes it hellishly confusing to remember. I hope I can remember their names on the day of the exam. LD. Lysander, Demetrius.'

Becca patted his arm. 'Just remember your goldfish,' she said. 'You'll be fine.'

Mac grimaced. 'Hope so. I'll be so happy when these

exams are out the way as I think I may be going slightly bonkers with stress.'

'So what happens next?' asked Cat. 'And who are all those artisans you mentioned?'

'They provide the sub-plot. They're a bunch of guys who get together to do plays,' said Mac. 'Like an am-dram group and they want to do a special play for the royal wedding. And as always with those type of groups, you always get one showoff who wants to play all the parts. In this play, it's a guy called Bottom.'

'Bottom?' asked Cat.

'Bottom,' Mac replied. 'Imagine if his surname was Cheek.'

'You *are* going bonkers,' said Becca.

'You may laugh,' said Mac, 'but there was a guy up at my school in London called Richard Pain.'

'So what's wrong with that?' asked Cat.

'We called him Dick for short. So he was Dick Pain.'

Cat and Becca groaned.

'To continue,' said Squidge, putting on a strict headteacher's voice. 'Now, as I said, Oberon and Titania have been arguing and Oberon wants revenge on Titania, so he tells his Head Fairy, Puck, to get some magic love flower juice and rub it into Titania's eyes when she's asleep, so that she falls in love with the first person she sees when she wakes up. And then he instructs Puck to make sure the first person she sees is one ugly dude. Puck takes this on board and when he sees Bottom showing off at the rehearsal, he decides to give him a donkey's head. Literally. Bottom, with his ridiculous clown head, gets lost in the woods, Titania wakes up and bingo, sees the donkey creature, falls in love with him and invites him to her flowery bed-type hammock thing in the trees. Oberon sees it all and thinks that it's hysterical because Titania is all over the donkey like a rash and all he wants is a bucket of oats and hay.'

'Cool,' said Becca. 'A person could have a lot of fun with that love potion.'

'And they do,' said Squidge. 'Puck puts it in Lysander's eyes and he sees Helena and falls in love with her and then Puck puts it in Demetrius's eyes and he falls back in love with Helena. She thinks they're all taking the mickey and mocking her and Hermia gets well upset because she thinks that no one fancies her any more.'

'What a mess,' said Cat. 'I think you should go as Puck, Squidge.'

'Yeah, maybe. Or the donkey,' said Squidge. 'I can't exactly do the Demetrius–Lysander look can I? I mean, when did you last see a Greek god type on crutches?'

* * *

The following week we were transported to *A Midsummer Night's Dream, à la* Axford.

Becca and Cat came over to my house to get ready early on Saturday evening. It was a tradition now that for any of Mum's dos that they came over and we got dressed together. For me, it was sometimes the best part of the party, trying on clothes, shoes and jewellery and doing each other's make-up. I really appreciated having Cat and Bec as friends down here because when Mum held an event in previous years, unless I had a mate down from my London school, I was often on my own and had no one to talk to, not only beforehand, but also when the party got going.

'Mac has just arrived,' said Cat as she peeked out of the window in the guest bedroom down into the courtyard below.

'As Demetrius?' I asked.

Cat nodded. 'Hairy legs and all.'

Becca took a peek then laughed. 'Someone should have told him that socks *and* sandals is not a good look. Never mind. He still looks cute.'

'He came up and picked his cossie last night,' I said. 'I thought he'd go for Demetrius as he fancies himself as a bit of a ladykiller.'

'Not in those socks,' said Cat.

'Who's Squidge coming as?' asked Becca.

'Still not sure,' I said. 'He wouldn't tell me. He wants it to be a surprise.'

'Bet he comes as the donkey,' said Cat. 'You know what he's like. Anything for a laugh.'

'*My Oberon . . . methought I was enamour'd of an ass*,' Becca quoted from the play. 'That's the line that Titania comes out with when she wakes up from her dream.'

'Great quote,' said Cat. 'And I bet a million girls all over the world have said something similar when they have awoken from some stupid infatuation with a boy. That Shakespeare stuff still works today doesn't it?'

'Yeah,' said Becca. 'But I guess that they had love affairs back then, too.'

We began to root through the costumes that were left on the rail in the guest room. Cat pulled out a Grecian dress and handed it to Becca.

'That would really suit you,' she said as Becca held it up against her in the mirror. 'Dead glam. If you put your hair up you'll look like a total goddess.'

'You think? You must say thanks to your mum, Lia, she's so brill getting all these costumes for us.'

'No prob,' I said. 'It isn't any extra work because her friend Daisy Oldfield runs a costume hire shop in Chelsea, so Mum just calls her and she sends a van of clothes down.'

'Thank her all the same,' said Cat. 'I wouldn't want her to think that we take it for granted. She's always shelling out for stuff for us.'

'I will, but you'd be the same if it were you,' I said. 'Anyway, she likes to do it.'

Mum was always great when it came to costumes for her parties. She was sensitive to the fact that none of my new friends came from a well-off background and so, to save any embarrassment, she always made sure that she got a selection of costumes in. 'For those who haven't the time to go looking or haven't a costume shop near them,' she had said diplomatically when the van from Daisy's had arrived on the Wednesday before the party.

'OK,' said Becca. 'So let's decide finally. Are you going as Hermia, Cat?'

'Don't think so. With my short hair, I'm hardly going to look like a Greek babe, am I? No, I want to go as Puck . . .'

'Good idea. Here,' said Becca and she pulled out a green pair of tights and a red jerkin and handed them to her. 'And you, Lia, you have to be Titania so that leaves me . . . Shall I go as Helena, the flighty airhead?'

'Definitely,' said Cat, and Becca punched her playfully on the arm.

'Star must be going as Titania as well,' I said as I flicked through the rails. 'I'm sure there were two Queen of the Fairies outfits here when they arrived.'

'That will be OK,' said Cat. 'You can be sister fairies.'

Becca pulled the Fairy Queen dress out and held it up against me. It was a wisp of soft green chiffon with silver sequins sewn into the skirt. Very pretty and elegant. 'This is definitely for you, Lia,' she said. 'It's got your name on it.'

I slipped the dress on and it did look fab, plus it fitted like a glove. We spent the next half-hour trying on various costumes but, in the end, went back to our original choices. After fixing our hair and doing our make-up, we emerged downstairs to join the arriving guests.

Cat looked divine as a pixie-style Puck. She'd spiked her hair with gel, applied loads of dark kohl round her eyes and wore purple lipstick, which made her look like a Goth fairy. Becca was a Greek goddess in a long toga dress with her hair pulled back off her face. I wore the fairy dress and my hair loose over my shoulders. I felt like a total Barbie doll, but the girls reassured me that it didn't look too naff.

Dad was standing at the bottom of the stairs dressed in

his Theseus outfit of a short toga with a crown of ivy on his head. He looked up and beamed when he saw us. 'Watch out, boys,' he said. 'You three look stunning.'

'You don't look bad yourself, Mr Axford,' said Becca. I had to laugh. Becca is such a flirt, even with my dad!

'Any idea who the boys are going as?' I asked.

Dad shook his head. 'They said they wanted it to be a surprise. But I reckon they'll go as Greek gods so they'll look handsome, and these togas give us lads a chance to show off our legs.'

Outside, cars were beginning to arrive and guests drifted into the hall and then out into the back where the party was to be held. The back terraces looked amazing. Mum, who was dressed like a Greek goddess, had instructed the decorators to create a grotto and so they had strewn ropes of fairy lights across the bushes and trees. Greek statues and pillars stood among the bushes and palm plants and tables were adorned with urns, flowers and fruit. Waiters (dressed as satyrs) and waitresses (dressed as fairies) took out drinks and canapés to a background sound of flute-playing. Even Max and Molly had garlands of leaves around their necks. The whole effect was enchanting.

'I feel like I'm in fairyland,' said Becca, as one of the waiters handed her a non-alcoholic cocktail.

'Me too,' said Cat, then she nudged me. 'Eyes left. The boys have arrived.'

I looked over to the rose arch at the entrance of the grotto and there were Ollie, Jamie, Henry and Michael. As Dad had predicted, they had all opted for the toga costumes and looked every inch the Greek gods. They looked handsome with their oiled muscles glistening in the soft light. Even some of the older female guests were ogling them.

'I don't believe it,' said Cat as they came over to join us. 'Look! Look at your arms and legs. You shaved!'

Ollie groaned. 'Shaved! I wish. No. We wanted to look a hundred per cent the part so Mum booked us in with her beautician. She's just finished. She *waxed* us. Talk about torture. I've never known pain like it. I will never ever complain about having to shave again now that I know what you girls go through.'

Suddenly, Cat burst out laughing and pointed at Jamie's legs. One was smooth, the other was hairy.

'It was too painful,' he said with a sheepish grin. 'I couldn't go through with it on both legs!'

'You have to suffer to be beautiful,' said Becca, then laughed as the boys did look slightly traumatised.

Half an hour later, most of the guests had arrived but

there was no sign of Squidge. I tried his mobile and it was switched off. I presumed that he was on his way.

And then we heard the sound of laughter from inside.

'I bet that's Squidge,' I said as I strained to see over people's heads. 'I *knew* he'd come as the donkey.'

The laughter grew closer and a strange figure made a grand entrance through the french windows and on to the terrace.

It was Squidge. He hadn't come as the ass. He'd come as Titania, Queen of the Fairies, in full make-up, with an auburn wig, big meringue-skirted dress that covered his broken leg and an ostrich-feather boa round his neck.

Cat burst out laughing. '*Totally* pantomime dame,' she said. 'Brill. Move over, Widow Twankey.'

'Dahlings,' said Squidge as he spotted us across the terrace, giving us a regal wave with his good hand.

I looked across at Michael Bradley with his smooth perfect limbs and his handsome face then back to Squidge in his ridiculous costume with red lips and way too much eye make-up.

I knew who I would prefer to be with any day.

15 Midsummer Meltdown

IN THE EARLY PART OF THE EVENING, everything was fantastic and everyone seemed to be having a whale of a time. Champagne was flowing for the adults, non-alcoholic punch for the teens. After a buffet supper, an area was cleared of tables, turned into a dance floor and music blared out from speakers that had been placed up in the trees. We were lucky that we didn't have neighbours and we could play music as loud as we liked into the early hours of the morning without anyone complaining.

The DJ began with a compilation of tracks from the Sixties and then on came the Seventies hit 'YMCA' where everyone goes loony and acts out the letters with their arms.

'Oh, I love this,' said Henry as he leapt about in time to the music. 'Where's Becca, love of my life?'

'Loo,' said Cat.

'Oh, then you come and dance with me,' he said and pulled her on to the dancefloor. 'Y . . . M . . . C . . . A.'

'I think he's been at the punch,' I said to Squidge as we watched Henry splay his arms and legs all over the place.

'Yeah,' said Squidge. 'I had some. Methinks it may be somewhat loaded *avec un* extra ingredient, courtesy of your brother.'

'What extra ingredient?'

'Bottle of vodka,' said Squidge. 'I saw him pour it in. Want some? 'Squite nice.'

I shook my head. 'Think I'll stick with my Coke. Alcohol always gives me a headache.'

'Does Cat want *all* the guys?' asked Becca when she came back and saw Cat on the dancefloor. 'First Ollie then Jamie and now *Henry* . . .'

'I don't think it's like that,' I said. 'You'd gone to the Ladies so he asked her. He said this track is one of his favourites.'

'Huh,' said Becca and flounced over to the bar area where she knocked back a punch drink, found Jamie, dragged him out on to the dancefloor and, when the music changed to a ballad, started smooch dancing with him.

'Oops,' I said as I watched them.

'Yeah. Oops,' said Squidge.

Cat finished dancing with Henry and came back to join Squidge and me, from where she watched Becca drape herself all over Jamie.

'Does Becca fancy Jamie now?' she asked.

'No. Least don't think so. You were dancing with Henry and I think she took the hump and . . .'

'Huh!' said Cat and grabbed Ollie to go and dance with her.

'What's got into Bec and Cat?' asked Squidge. 'I thought that Becca and Henry were an item and that Cat was into Jamie.'

'So did I. Maybe someone's put some of that magic potion stuff into their eyes,' I replied.

'Yeah, maybe,' said Squidge. 'Think it might be the punch though. Punch! Hah. That's a good name for it because it does pack a punch . . .' He went to act out throwing a punch with his good hand and one of his crutches swayed and he almost slipped.

'Woahhhhh, oops,' he said as he steadied himself.

'You OK?' I asked. 'How much punch have you had?'

'Only three glasses. So do you want to dance?'

'Dance? But you can't . . . your leg . . .'

'No such word as "can't",' said Squidge with a wide grin and hobbled out on to the dancefloor.

His dancing was a show stopper and after a few moments other dancers moved to the edge of the dancefloor and watched him. Me included, as if I stayed too close I was in danger of being stabbed in the foot with a crutch.

'I think he may have invented a new dance form,' said Michael, appearing at my side.

'I know. And when he's not got a broken leg, he has a whole range of dances in his repertoire: Hawaiian, Spanish, alien, Russian, though I doubt he'll be doing Russian tonight. At least I hope not or else he'll end up with two broken legs.'

Michael laughed, put his arm round me and gave me a hug. 'You really like him, don't you?'

I nodded.

Michael gave me a kiss on my forehead. 'In Morocco, I said Squidge was lucky to have you, but I can see why you like him. He seems like a great guy.'

I took his hand and gave it a squeeze. 'Thanks, Michael,' I said. 'He is.'

Michael sauntered off and I looked back at the dancefloor. Squidge had stopped dancing and was watching me. He hobbled over. 'What was that all about?'

'Just Michael saying that he thought you looked like a great guy.'

'Yeah, right. And that's why he kissed you?'

'Kiss? That wasn't a real kiss. It was a peck. A friendly peck. I think he's glad I'm with you.'

Squidge turned away so that I couldn't see his face but I felt my insides turn over. He didn't believe me.

'I'm telling you the truth, Squidge. I said I would and I am. Come on, don't be jealous. You soooo don't need to be . . .'

Squidge took a deep breath and turned back. 'Sorry. Just . . . I can't help but be jealous and . . . pfff . . . I know I look a bit of a prat tonight compared to the Greek gods over there.'

'And *that's* why I love you. You're geeeorgeous,' I said and gave him a big kiss on his scarlet lips.

'Sorry,' he said. 'I know. Call me Mr Stupoid. I . . . I guess there's part of me still can't believe that you're with me.'

'You're *mental*. You're easily the most interesting guy here.'

Squidge looked down at his dress, adjusted his false bosoms and flicked his auburn hair back over his shoulder. 'You think?' he said in a really girlie way.

'Oh definitely,' I replied. 'And *soooo* manly.'

Cat came over and nudged me. 'Hey, George has put

together a slide show from Morocco. Want to see it? It's showing in the library.'

'Oh, we *have* to see this,' said Squidge. 'See how it compares to your pics. You coming?'

'Yeah, course.' I nodded and followed him and Cat into the house.

The show had already started and images from Marrakech played on the screen. There were some great shots. The hotel. The roof terrace. Various portrait shots of guests. Everyone having a laugh.

In the dark, I took Squidge's hand. 'I sooo wished you were there. I really hope you believe that.'

'I do now,' he said. 'And I'm sorry about before.'

Vibrant shots of the market appeared. Stalls selling spices and jewellery and pots and cedarwood boxes and herbs. And then came a series of photos from the Fantasia night. The Berber tribesmen, the horses, the girls with their rose petals, the tents, the performers and then some of the finale. Guests watching the display at the end. The horses charging. The fireworks lighting up the sky.

And then I froze in horror.

Up there on the screen was a shot of the crowd. Upturned faces watching the sky except for two people in the left-hand corner.

It was Michael and me.

I had my eyes closed and I was being kissed. Clear as anything. On the lips.

Both Squidge and I gasped as the slide show went on to the next slide.

'No, Squidge, it was . . . let me explain . . .'

But he'd already got up and was putting his crutches under his arms. 'Truth, huh? And I suppose you're going to tell me that *that* was an innocent peck as well?'

'*No. Yes* . . . Please . . .'

But Squidge was already up on his feet and hobbling through the assembled guests. I got up to follow him. He was in such a rush to get out that he tripped on someone's bag and went down. A dozen guests rushed to help him including Michael who had been standing at the back watching the slide show. I felt awful as I watched him splayed out in front of me. He looked so helpless lying there on the floor. He glanced up at me with such a look, a cross between hurt, vulnerability and accusation.

'I'm OK,' he said as he struggled to get up. 'I'm OK. I'm OK.'

But he couldn't stand on his own. He needed the hands that reached out to help him up and I could see that he was hating every single second as four guys hoisted him to his feet.

George was one of them. 'Which way, boss?' he asked.

'Out . . .' blustered Squidge. 'Home. I got to get home. Car park. Home.'

I scoured the library for Cat and saw that she was on the other side of the room. She had seen everything and came rushing over.

'He saw you on the slide?' she asked.

I nodded. 'I think everyone did. Will you come after him with me? Will you explain?'

She nodded and we ran out to the car park where we saw Squidge talking into his mobile and limping off as fast as he could.

'Squidge . . .' she called. 'Wait up . . .'

He hobbled faster.

We ran after him and caught him up.

'Oh come on, Squidge,' Cat called. 'Give Lia a chance. I know you saw the slide but I was there. Nothing happened. Not really.'

Squidge stopped and turned to look at us. 'You knew? Jesus, Cat . . . You *all* knew . . . And . . . you know what, I knew too. I *knew* something had happened.'

'Well, you'd be wrong,' said Cat. 'Not everyone knew because *nothing* happened?'

'Yeah, right, and that's why there's a slide showing Michael kissing Lia. When were you going to tell me, Lia?' said Squidge, turning to me. 'Jesus, what an ass I've been to think that you really cared. Go on, get back in there, get back to your rich boyfriend.'

'Oh, for God's sake, Squidge,' shouted Cat. 'Grow *up*. You have such an almighty chip on your shoulder I'm amazed that you can walk at all, never mind the crutches!'

'She told me that nothing went on in Morocco,' said Squidge.

'It didn't. Michael and I are just friends,' I said. 'I told you the *truth*.'

'*Very* good friends by the looks of the slide. And everyone saw them. I always *knew* this would happen one day. You'd find out that I'm not good enough for you. But when were you going to tell *me*?'

For a moment I felt like bursting out laughing. Squidge was still in full fairy queen outfit, full pantomime dame gear and he looked *so* petulant. And then I couldn't help it. I *did* laugh. And so did Cat.

Squidge gave us both such a filthy look.

'Oh come on, Squidge,' said Cat. 'I mean, look at you!'

But he didn't laugh. Or even smile.

'I'll leave you to sort things out with Widow Twankey here,' Cat said and then turned to go back to the house. *'Lord, what fools these mortals be!'*

Squidge began to limp off at full speed in the other direction. I ran after him.

'Oh please, Squidge. Come on. You have to see the funny side of this,' I pleaded. 'What's happened to your sense of humour?'

'Gone down the drain, like our relationship.'

'Oh please don't be like this. Please . . .'

'I'd always felt that there was something you were holding back from me and now I know I was right.'

'OK. So Michael kissed me. A kiss. It meant *nothing*. I didn't tell you *because* it didn't mean anything and I didn't want it blown out of proportion . . .'

'But we *promised* to tell each other the truth even if it hurt,' said Squidge. *'Remember?'*

'I do,' I said.

'OK. Then if it's truth time then here's one for *you*. You're not the only one with secrets. I met someone when you were away.'

For a moment I felt like he had stabbed me. '*You?* What, in the hospital?'

'Yeah.'

'Who?'

'One of the nurses.'

'No. You're making this up.'

'No, I'm not.'

'OK. What's her name?'

'Colette. Colette Armstrong. And I'm going to see her *right* now,' said Squidge and hobbled off. 'At least I can trust her.'

I watched him limp off into the night hoping that he'd turn around and come back.

But he didn't.

Bath, Bed, Boring 16

CAT BURST OUT LAUGHING. 'Colette Armstrong?' she asked. 'Colette *Armstrong*! Are you sure?'

I nodded. 'Absolutely. Why? Do you know her?'

'Duh,' said Cat. 'She lives down the street from us.'

'And is she like a mega-babe-type nurse?'

Cat started laughing again. 'Er . . . not exactly. She's about fifty. *Very* large. Bit of a moustache and hairy legs – I know this because she rides, or rather wobbles, around on her bicycle and everyone can see her shins. Oh . . . and she's got five kids and a husband.'

'Oh, I know her,' said Becca. 'Lady with frizzy grey hair?' Cat nodded.

Becca began laughing too. 'Ah, then I don't think you have to worry about the competition,' she said.

'So why would Squidge mention her?' I asked.

'Temporary insanity. Heat of the moment,' said Cat. 'He was hurt and he wanted to lash out. And there is some truth in it. He does see her regularly as she is the nurse who does all the home visits so she'll have been keeping an eye on his dressings and so on.'

'I'll kill him,' I said. And then I started to see the funny side as well. 'I will. I'll really kill him.'

Later that night, when all the guests had gone home after the party, I went to my computer and wrote Squidge an e-mail.

Dearest Squidge,
Thanks for telling me about your new lover Colette. I hope that you will be very happy together. And I hope that her husband and five children don't mind too much that you are having a love affair under their noses.

I'm so sorry that I didn't tell you that Michael kissed me in Morocco. It was really stupid of me, especially as it meant nothing. I didn't tell you

because I didn't want it to be an issue
but now it is and I wish I'd told you
the truth in the first place. It's a
real lesson to me not to hold back. I
held back for fear of hurting you and
ended up hurting you more and for that
I am truly sorry.

Please can we start again? You are the
only boy I want to be with. I don't care
that your family aren't rich or famous.
Why would I? They are great people and
that's what counts. And I think you are
exceptional.

I hope to see you really, really soon.

Yours,

Li@ XXXXX

I sent it off and went to bed in the hope that he'd see it
first thing in the morning and we'd get back to normal as
soon as possible. I was so tired after all the ups and downs
of the day that I fell asleep the second my head hit the
pillow, and even slept through my alarm clock. As soon as
I did wake up, I went straight to the computer to see if I
had mail.

There was one.

Dear Li@,

I'm sorry about last night too. It was weird all round. Listen, as you know, this is the big two weeks for my GCSEs and I won't be in school much, apart from to do my exams, so it's likely that I won't see you around much. I want to do well in these exams and so . . . I hope you understand but I'd like to take some time out and focus on my work. So maybe no calls either. Last night really did my head in and when I feel like that, I can't think straight and I need to for the next couple of weeks if I'm going to get through.

And then, well, let's just see how the summer goes.

Hope you understand.

Bye for now,

Squidge

I gasped. He hadn't even signed off love Squidge. And no kisses. When we first got together, he'd write millions of XXXs.

I quickly pressed 'reply' and wrote:

   I understand. Good luck with the exams.
   Li@ X

I didn't understand, though. I knew that Squidge took his
work seriously but, like everything else in his life, he
usually managed to make it fun, like he'd take his books
out to some gorgeous spot on the peninsula and he'd revise
and I'd do my homework or read. Or he'd come up here and
lie on my bed and work and then I'd test him and if he got
the right answers, I'd feed him Jelly Babies or Liquorice
Allsorts. Or like the other night when we all watched *A
Midsummer Night's Dream* together and he went over the
plot and characters for us.

   But I knew there was no more to say. I had said I was
sorry. I had done my best to explain. I had to respect his
request and there was nothing more that I could do until
his exams were over.

The following week, life went back to normal. School.
Home. Homework. Telly. Bath. Bed. Boring. And I missed
Squidge like crazy.

   I saw Cat and Becca at school and occasionally we caught
sight of the Year Eleven boys going in or coming out of the
hall, which had been set up as the main exam place.

   'Hey, Mac. How's it going?' asked Cat on Friday

morning when we bumped into him as he was going down the corridor to the main hall.

Mac shrugged. 'Hard to tell. Some have been better than others.'

'Er . . . seen Squidge?' I asked.

'Yeah.'

'How's he doing?'

'OK. He's getting around better every day. He . . . er told me that you were taking a break from each other.'

'Yeah. But . . . has he said anything to you about how he feels now? He asked me not to call.'

Mac shifted uncomfortably on his feet and I felt bad that I'd put him on the spot. 'Not really,' said Mac. 'Only that he needed to keep a clear head until, you know, until it's all over . . .'

'Yeah, but after that?'

Mac shrugged.

'What she wants to know is if he's going to dump her,' said Becca. 'Come on, I bet you know.'

Mac sighed heavily. 'Look. I know that it's none of my business but he's really got it into his stupid, thick head that he's not good enough for you. Not in your league and that, one day, you're going to find out so best to end it now before that happens.'

'Idiot,' I said.

'Thanks,' said Mac. 'I was only trying to help.'

'Not you. Him.'

'Oh. Right.'

'So what do you think I should do?'

'His last exam is a week today. If you do care about him, do something at the weekend after he's finished. His curfew will be over then so he hasn't got any more excuses to avoid you, so get down and see him. Sort it out.'

'She will,' said Becca. 'And good luck for the rest of your exams.'

'Thanks,' said Mac. 'Better go.'

'So what are you going to do?' asked Cat as we made our way down to our classroom and Mac headed for the exam hall.

'I think you should go down and see him and give him a good thumping until he sees sense,' said Becca.

'What? Beat up a boy with a broken leg?'

'Yeah. Well, I could bash him myself, he's so stupid. If he's not careful, he's going to lose you.'

'Or I'm going to lose him.'

'I know what you should do,' said Cat.

'What?'

'Do a Squidge.'

'A Squidge?'

'Yeah,' said Cat. 'Don't just go down there and try to talk him around. Do something spectacular . . . you know . . . a Squidge.'

I nodded. I knew exactly what she meant by 'doing a Squidge'. Last time we'd had a falling out, instead of coming up to the house and trying to resolve things, he'd decorated his back garden with fairy lights, got Cat, Becca and Mac to dress up as cinema attendants and invited me to a private showing of one of my favourite movies. And the first time we ever kissed, he planned it down to the last detail – location, lighting, everything. Instead of doing it on a street corner or on a front porch, he'd carted a rucksack full of candles up to a tiny church on the edge of the peninsula in the early evening and lit the place with candlelight. It was so romantic.

He'd explained once that he had this idea about life. That we go and watch movies and so on, but often don't realise that actually we are in a movie of our own and we get to choose what role we play: hero or victim. We make up the script and our own dialogue. We do the casting – choose our friends, who we want as leading man or woman. And we get to choose the locations. To a degree, he'd added. We'll be able to choose more when we leave school. But he said that he wanted to live his life as if he was a film director of his own film and make it the best movie he could. Hence the kissing scene. He wanted it to be memorable. And hence the fairy garden for after our falling out. That was memorable too. Things like that were 'doing a Squidge'.

'I know what you mean,' I said, and it felt like a light pinged on in my head. 'And I think I know exactly what we could do.'

'What?' asked Becca.

'Squidge missed out on the Morocco trip, yeah? OK. So we're going to bring Morocco to him.'

'Great idea,' said Cat then looked blank. 'Er . . . but how exactly?'

It took some planning and I had to move fast because I had only a week.

First I called Ollie and asked him to send me the CD of Moroccan music he'd bought in Marrakech.

Then I went into Plymouth with Cat and Becca and bought a DVD called *Learn How to Bellydance* and I spent hours practising everywhere: in the bathroom, while I had my breakfast, in my room.

Dad agreed to set up a tent on the private beach on the edge of our estate. In fact, he and Mum were brilliant and really got into the idea. Mum was straight on the phone to her friend Daisy and had a pile of Moroccan costumes sent down for us all. Then they spent all day Saturday down on the beach helping us get things ready. Dad and Mac put the tent up and then Mum and Meena furnished the tent with cushions and lamps and rugs taken from various parts of the house. It looked totally brilliant by the time they'd finished. Just like the tents at the Fantasia. Dad built a fire, ready for when Squidge arrived, and Meena cooked up some fab Moroccan food: a lamb tagine and roasted vegetables and couscous. And when Mum lit some of the cinnamon joss sticks she'd bought at the market in Marrakech, I felt myself transported back there.

Squidge's dad was in on the secret too, because we needed someone to drive Squidge as close to the beach as possible.

'He's going to love this,' Mr Squires said when we spoke on the phone. 'He needs a lift. He's been like a bear with a sore head, never mind a sore leg, since you two stopped seeing each other. Count me in. I'll have him there at seven on the dot.'

And so the stage was set. An empty beach with an empty tent.

It looked so serene. The weather was lovely. The scent of

spices filled the air. The tagine gently cooking on the fire. Mum, Cat, Becca and I were dressed in traditional Moroccan costume and Dad and Mac as Berber tribesmen.

In the distance, we could see Mr Squires's pick-up van making its way down on to the beach.

'Everyone hide,' said Dad.

'It's OK,' I said. 'I told Mr Squires to blindfold Squidge.'

A few minutes later, we saw Mr Squires leading Squidge down the narrow lane to the beach. He saw us and gave us the thumbs up.

I gave Mac the signal and he pressed 'play' on the CD player and the sound of Moroccan music filled the air.

Mr Squires led Squidge to the front of the tent and then inside, where at last he took off his blindfold. Squidge sniffed the air, looked around him.

I gave everyone the signal and we all appeared at the front of the tent and bowed low.

'Greetings, Master,' I said. 'And welcome to Morocco.'

Squidge's face broke into the biggest smile.

'Please be seated, o Master,' said Mac with a bow, and Mr Squires helped his son sit back among the cushions. A moment later, Meena appeared with a tray with a glass of fresh orange juice on it and some lovely Moroccan nibbles with goat's cheese and olives.

And then the entertainment began. First was Dad and his juggling act — with tennis balls. He wasn't very good and kept dropping them, but Squidge seemed to enjoy it all the same.

Next was Mac, who did some magic card tricks.

Then came Becca, who sang a very strange song which sounded like she was being strangled, and Squidge put his fingers in his ears and begged her to stop.

Cat's act followed and she did her level best to do some interesting acrobatics, but fell over when she attempted a handstand.

By this time, Squidge looked like he was having the time of his life, and was laughing his head off.

I quickly went round the back of the tent and got into my belly dancer outfit and yashmak.

Mac's head appeared round the back of the tent a few minutes later. 'Ready? Everyone's in the tent with Squidge now.'

I nodded. He disappeared and a moment later the sound of music started up again.

I took a deep breath and went round to the front, where I began to dance. To begin with, I didn't dare look at anyone. And then as the music swelled, I really got into it. Forget you have an audience, I thought. Just dance. And it felt amazing. As I turned round, in front of me was the ocean. The sun setting in the distance lighting the sky pink, red and orange. To my right, the fire crackled, the sand felt warm beneath my feet and, for a moment, I didn't feel like Lia Axford. Daughter of Zac Axford. Little Miss Boring. I felt at one with all that was around me, dancing in a timeless moment. I moved in time to the music and felt that I could have been anywhere in the world.

As the music faded then stopped, I finally glanced into the tent.

Squidge looked like his eyes were going to fall out of his head. Mum had a big stupid grin on her face and Dad just beamed then started clapping.

He got up and nodded at the others. 'Come on, guys, let's leave them alone for a while. I've got some drinks up at the house for you and we can come back down later.'

Cat and Becca got up and followed Dad then Cat turned back and gave me the thumbs up.

When they'd gone, I went into the tent and sat at Squidge's feet.

'O Lord Squires, sheik of Barton Hall Beach and master of all in the Rame peninsula. I beseech you. Have mercy upon the poor lost soul of Lia Axford. Although an ordinary girl and from humble origins, she has a true heart and has learned her lesson well. She has learned that it is important to tell the truth no matter what.'

Squidge lay back on the cushions. 'Hhlımm. Has she now? Tell o yonder girl that I will consider her case. But she may need to beg somewhat more.'

'Somewhat more? Oh! OK. What does my master desire?'

'He desireth . . . oh for heaven's sake, come here, Lia,' said Squidge as he held out his good arm to me.

I went and cuddled up to him in our makeshift Moroccan tent and together we gazed out at the ocean. As the light from the fire grew brighter against the darkening sky, I thought that it couldn't get any better. I didn't need to be in a five-star hotel in some faraway exotic location. I had all that I wanted right here. As long as Squidge and I were together, any place was fine by me.

The complete Cathy Hopkins collection

The MATES, DATES series

The TRUTH, DARE, KISS, PROMISE series

The CINNAMON GIRL series

Find out more at www.piccadillypress.co.uk
Join Cathy's Club at www.cathyhopkins.com

Cathy Hopkins

Like this book?
Become a mate today!